SHOWDOWN AT EAGLE'S NEST

SHOWDOWN AT EAGLE'S NEST

by

L. D. Tetlow

Dales Large Print Books
Long Preston, North Yorkshire,
BD23 4ND, England.

British Library Cataloguing in Publication Data.

Tetlow, L. D.
　　Showdown at Eagle's Nest.

　　A catalogue record of this book is
　　available from the British Library

　　ISBN　1-84262-192-0 pbk

First published in Great Britain in 2001 by Robert Hale Limited

Copyright © L. D. Tetlow 2001

The right of L. D. Tetlow to be identified as the author of this work has been asserted by him in accordance with the Copyright, Designs and Patents Act, 1988

Published in Large Print 2002 by arrangement with Robert Hale Limited

Dales Large Print is an imprint of Library Magna Books Ltd.

Printed and bound in Great Britain by
T.J. (International) Ltd., Cornwall, PL28 8RW

ONE

Caleb Black, part-time preacher and full-time bounty hunter, black by both colour and name, rode slowly down the main street of the small town of Beresford uncertain as to the reception he would receive. He did not normally bother about what kind of reception he would receive, but on this occasion people in the street stopped and stared with looks almost akin to hatred. Strange looks and obvious curiosity were reactions to which he was quite accustomed and he noted that there did not appear to be another black face in town. Again, there was nothing unusual in that and it did at least explain the interest in him but it did not explain the pure hostility he felt.

He could not help but smile as he saw mothers clutching their children close and whispering to them. He could well imagine that the children were being threatened that he would take them away and eat them if they did not behave. That was about the most common threat which, he well knew, stemmed from the old belief that all negroes were descended from cannibals. Whatever was said, it did appear to have an effect on the behaviour of various children. Half-way down the street a man displaying the badge of a sheriff on his shirt stepped out and flagged him down.

'Are you lookin' for somethin'?' demanded the sheriff.

'Accommodation, a meal and a bath,' replied Caleb. 'The Reverend Caleb Black, at your service, Sheriff.'

'Reverend!' said the sheriff. 'Sure, you dress like a preacher, but that don't mean much. Preachers an' gamblers all dress pretty much the same. Anyhow, we ain't got no use for another preacher in town. Our regular minister is Mr Wilberforce an' I don't think he'll take too kindly to havin' competition.'

'It was not my intention to set up a rival ministry,' said Caleb, dismounting and leading his horse to a hitching rail outside the sheriff's office. 'I have been travelling for almost a week and am in need of some decent food and a bath. I think a bath would be first on my list. Perhaps you could direct me to someone who provides such a service. I shall be on my way in a few days.'

The sheriff looked Caleb up and down and sneered. 'I don't know how you folk know when you're clean or dirty, it sure don't show you bein' the colour you are an' that's a fact.'

'Perhaps it is not quite so obvious to the eye of a white man,' replied Caleb. He had heard all such remarks many times and they had long since ceased to have any effect on him. 'However, despite what many white folk might believe, we do have feelings and we do know when we are dirty. I take it that there are no other black people living in Beresford.'

'Fancy talker too,' said the sheriff. 'I ain't never met a black feller what's had a good education before. No, Reverend, as far as I know there ain't no other … er … blacks within a hundred miles, barrin' one.'

'Bar one?' asked Caleb.

'Yeh, bar one,' said the sheriff. 'I reckon most folk round here think you've come to join him. There sure don't seem no other reason for a black feller to come to these parts. You're a long way from your home in the South. Are you a runaway slave?'

'I was born a free man in the North,' replied Caleb. 'It is true that my father was a slave but that's all. As a matter of fact I served with the US cavalry in the rank of lieutenant.'

'Lieutenant!' said the sheriff, plainly surprised and disbelieving. 'I ain't never heard of a black officer before.'

'There were very few of us,' said Caleb. 'We served with purely black units. It was felt, probably correctly, that white soldiers would refuse to serve under us even in the so-called liberated North.'

'OK,' said the sheriff, 'I'll buy that. I do seem to remember somethin' about black-only units. I never saw any but then I never saw what they called the Camel Corps either. In fact I don't even know what a camel is.'

'Strange-looking animals, taller than horses but with a great hump on their backs,' said Caleb. 'They tried using them because they can go for many days without water and are ideal in the desert. I think they come from countries which have lots of deserts. I don't think the idea was a great success. I seem to remember they disbanded it eventually.'

'Yeh, well, anyhow, I can guarantee that most folk think you're here to join Black Bill.'

'And why should they think that?' asked Caleb.

'On account of he's the only other black man in this territory an' a no-good outlaw,' said the sheriff. 'Goes by the name of Williams, Courtney Williams, better known as Black Bill. He leads a small band of outlaws, four of 'em, three whites an' one half-breed Sioux.'

'Outlaws!' said Caleb. 'Perhaps I might be of help. I specialize in saving the souls of outlaws.'

The sheriff laughed. 'Reverend, folk round here don't give a shit about savin' nobody's soul 'ceptin' their own an' they sure don't care what the hell happens to men like Black Bill. I'd ride on if I was you, I don't think Black Bill nor any of his men are interested in havin' their soul saved.'

'I think you misunderstand, Sheriff,' said Caleb. 'Perhaps we could talk in your office?'

'Sure,' replied the sheriff, looking at the crowd which had started to gather. 'Might be safer for you as well. See that big feller at the back?' Caleb looked and nodded. 'His wife was raped by Black Bill and his men last year. I don't think he would've bothered that much if it had just been the white fellers but havin' a black an' a half-breed go at her...? Well, puttin' it plainly, he's

11

promised to cut the balls off every black an' every half-breed he can.'

'And has he succeeded?' asked Caleb.

'Not yet, but I sure wouldn't like for him to be left alone with you.'

'Then I must make certain that I am never alone with him,' said Caleb, deliberately smiling at the man. The effect was to make the man turn purple with rage. The sheriff led the way into his office and closed the door. Almost immediately curious faces were pressing up against the window, including the big man's.

There was a young deputy in the office and the sheriff ordered him to go outside and disperse the crowd. Caleb ignored the comments which could be plainly heard and eventually the crowd moved away.

'So what do you want?' asked the sheriff when his deputy returned. 'Folk don't normally want to come into my office 'less they want somethin'.'

'I am curious about this Black Bill and his gang,' said Caleb. He slowly pulled aside his long coat to reveal a gun on each hip. The sheriff was plainly surprised and whistled softly. Caleb smiled and allowed his coat to fall back.

'Fine-lookin' pieces of hardware,' said the

sheriff. 'First time I ever seen a preacher wearin' guns. In fact it's the first time in many years since I seen any man wearin' two of 'em. You claim to be a preacher but lookin' at you I'd say you was a man who knew exactly how to use them pieces. I'm curious, tell me more.'

'I do know exactly how to use them,' said Caleb. 'Perhaps it would be as well if your man outside was aware of it. I have an aversion to being castrated.'

'I'll tell him,' said the sheriff. 'Last thing I want is any killin' in this town. So tell me, if you are a preacher, what's the purpose of fire-power like that?'

'I am indeed an ordained minister,' said Caleb, taking a paper out of his inside jacket pocket and handing it to the sheriff. 'As you can see, this is my authority to officiate in church ceremonies.' The sheriff read the paper, grunted and handed it back. 'Unfortunately, as I have no doubt your minister Mr … er…'

'Wilberforce,' reminded the sheriff.

'Wilberforce,' said Caleb. 'I have no doubt that he will confirm that earning a living as a minister is not the easiest way of life. There are many occasions when people will claim to need the services of a minister,

13

such as weddings, christenings and funerals but these occasions apart, they are never too keen to support a minister. Like many of my calling, I find it necessary to earn my living by other means. Most turn to things like carpentry or running a store of some kind. Since I am certainly not a carpenter and the thought of spending my life running a store does not appeal, I have turned to bounty hunting.'

'Bounty huntin'!' exclaimed the sheriff. 'Now I heard everythin'. I wouldn't've thought that kind of life would fit in with bein' a preacher. What the hell do you do, preach at 'em until they give themselves up?'

'Something along the lines of a sermon at ten paces?' said Caleb with a dry laugh. 'If it were as simple as that I certainly wouldn't require these guns. You might find it hard to believe, Sheriff, but I am quite prepared to kill a man if necessary. In fact I have killed quite a few and I do not find it conflicts with my beliefs in any way. Does not the Good Book advocate an eye for an eye? I am merely an instrument of the Lord's justice and vengeance.'

'I've heard of hell-fire preachers but this is the first time I ever met one what actually practises what he preaches an' I have to admit you scare the hell out of me,' said the sheriff.

'The innocent have nothing to fear from me,' assured Caleb. 'Now, to business, Sheriff. If this Black Bill and his men are known outlaws, I take it they all have rewards out on them?'

'Sure have,' said the sheriff, opening a drawer and pulling out five Wanted posters which he handed to Caleb. 'As you can see, Black Bill has seven hundred an' fifty on his head.'

'I've seen better rewards,' said Caleb, thumbing through the posters. 'Seven fifty, five hundred, two hundred, one hundred and fifty.' He looked at the poster marked $50 and smiled. 'He can't be very old.'

'A young eighteen-year-old tearaway called Jake Smith,' said the sheriff. 'Yeh, Smith. That's his real name. His folks used to live in Beresford but they died within two months of each other a couple of years back. Jake was a load of trouble even before they died but when he was left on his own he took up with Black Bill. So far he ain't done nothin' more serious than rob a few folk but I reckon it's only a matter of time before he kills somebody.'

15

'Then perhaps there is still hope for him,' said Caleb. 'Can I keep these posters? I'd like to get to know them better.'

'Sure,' replied the sheriff. 'They're pretty good likenesses of all of them, 'ceptin' maybe the half-breed, but then there ain't that many half-breeds in these parts so if you see one the chances are it's him.'

'And the others,' said Caleb, 'are they local?'

'Nope, they just sort of appeared,' replied the sheriff. He looked at Caleb curiously for a few moments. 'Are you for real, Reverend, are you thinkin' seriously about goin' after them? They won't be that easy to find, they know this country pretty well by now.'

'Sheriff,' said Caleb with a wry smile, 'the rewards from bounty hunting can be very good, but even we have our lean times and I have just been through a long period without earning anything. I have gone after men with higher rewards out on them and if there were any better prospects around I probably wouldn't bother. However sixteen hundred dollars is well worth expending a little effort. Where can I find this Black Bill?'

'Up in the Blue Mountains,' said the sheriff. 'That's the mountains north of here. Mind, if you was to hang about long enough they might just ride into town. They do sometimes.'

'Then why don't you arrest them when they do?' asked Caleb.

'On account of I like stayin' alive,' said the sheriff. 'I ain't no coward but five guns against one, maybe two if you count Ted here…' he nodded at his deputy, 'ain't the kind of odds I favour.'

'What about the other folk in town?' said Caleb. 'If they make a habit of raping women in town surely some of them would help?'

The sheriff laughed drily. 'Oh sure, they'll hold meetin's an' make all sorts of threatenin' noises, but that's all they are, noises. Even that big feller, Sam Boulton, suddenly finds he can't spare the time when it comes to it. If either me or Ted was to tackle them an' get shot they'd hold another meetin', say how sorry they were an' that it shouldn't be allowed to happen, but that's all. Sure, they'd probably all attend my funeral an' then argue about who to make sheriff but there ain't one of 'em what'd be prepared to take the job.'

'A common complaint amongst a lot of sheriffs,' said Caleb. 'I'll have to see what I can do. In the meantime I need a bath, a meal and somewhere to sleep.'

'The barber across the street does hot baths,' replied the sheriff. 'As for food an' somewhere to sleep there's the hotel a couple of doors down. The only problem is that Ben Casey who owns it is from the South an' I ain't too sure if he'll take negroes. I know he won't allow Indians or half-breeds in.'

'Perhaps he will take more notice of the colour of my money than my skin,' said Caleb with a sarcastic laugh. 'It's surprising just how many people have a change of heart when they see hard cash. Money is a great leveller in that it is the same if offered by a white man or a black man.'

'Maybe,' agreed the sheriff. 'Business has sure been slack of late. I'll talk to him first if you like, explain just who you are but I don't know if I'll make any difference.'

'Thank you,' said Caleb. 'However, I would appreciate if you didn't mention to anyone that I am a bounty hunter, at least not for the moment. I take it the barber does not mind if a black body dirties his water.'

'He'll be glad of the business,' said the sheriff. 'Like I said, things are pretty slack round here at the moment. The big cattle-drive finished a month ago. If you'd been here then you wouldn't've stood a chance, even if you are a preacher. OK, I won't tell nobody what your real business is, neither will Ted.' The deputy nodded in agreement. 'You can stable your horse down at the livery at the end of the street,' he continued, 'but I wouldn't leave your saddle or guns there, things like that have a habit of goin' missin'.'

Caleb thanked the sheriff and left the office. Before he tried the barber, he took his horse down to the livery where, somewhat grudgingly, the blacksmith agreed to take his horse. The charge was fifty cents a day, including feed and water. Remembering the sheriff's warning, Caleb removed the saddle and his rifle and carried them to the barber's shop. The barber, an elderly man, appeared only too happy that someone wanted to use his services and proved to be a very talkative man.

'Don't get many black folk in these parts,' said the barber as he filled a tub with hot water. 'Apart from Black Bill, we ain't seen a black face in more'n two years. Luke tells me you're a preacher.'

'Luke?' queried Caleb as he undressed, taking care not to show the barber that he wore two guns by wrapping them in his clothes. His rifle and saddle were placed in a corner of the room.

'The sheriff, Luke Solomons,' replied the barber. 'Seems he's taken a bit of a shine to you for some reason. I think he's persuaded Ben Casey to rent you a room an' Ben is a real dyed-in-the-wool Southerner to listen to him. He claims his family used to own slaves down there. I wouldn't take much notice of what he says though, he's all talk.'

'Just like that big man, Sam Boulton,' said Caleb with a wry smile.

'The difference is that Sam has one hell of a temper,' said the barber. 'It takes a lot to rile him but when he does snap there's no knowin' what he'll do. I reckon Luke told you what happened to his missus. Nasty business that an' Sam's made it pretty plain he's out to get all blacks an' half-breeds an' I think he means it.'

'Then I need to watch my back,' said Caleb as he climbed into the tub.

Caleb relaxed in the hot water for some time before soaping himself. In the meantime the barber maintained a steady chatter of meaningless talk, most of which Caleb could not remember. However, he did ask what the barber knew about Black Bill and his men.

'Not that much,' called the barber from

the adjoining room. 'Only one most folk know anythin' about is young Jake Smith. He grew up in this town an' was always a tearaway even when he was a boy. His folks died a couple of years back. They say that his mother took her own life after his pa died when a buggy fell down a ditch. I ain't so sure about that though, she never was a well woman. I think she just lost the will to live. Anyhow, shortly after that Jake took up with Black Bill.'

'And this Black Bill,' said Caleb, 'how long has he been around?'

'Let's see now,' said the barber, leaning against the door. 'It must be three years at least, maybe four. He just rode into town one day an' for a few weeks he warn't no bother. Then one day he robbed the general store an' since then he's been a thorn in everybody's side. The half-breed joined him first then two of the white fellers an' finally young Jake. Mostly they keep to robbin' the stage but sometimes they rob strangers. I hear tell that they've murdered at least ten strangers.'

'Ten!' exclaimed Caleb.

'That's what they say,' said the barber. 'Maybe it's just talk, I don't know. We get strangers an' drifters through from time to time but once they've left town nobody gives a shit what happens to 'em. There ain't no real way of knowin' if they killed 'em or not since nobody bothers to find out what happens when they do leave town. Personally I reckon it's all talk. It's a sure fact nobody ain't never discovered a body, 'ceptin' one an' he wasn't shot. The doc reckoned he broke his neck fallin' off his horse when he was drunk.'

'Even if they haven't killed all those men, I'm still surprised that nobody has tried to get rid of them,' said Caleb. 'Especially after they raped Sam Boulton's wife. I would have thought the whole town would have been up in arms.'

The barber laughed drily. 'Oh, they held a meetin' all right, made all the usual threats an' called upon Luke to do somethin' about it. He did try to form a posse but as is normal, although they all demanded action, there wasn't one of 'em prepared to actually do anythin' about it, 'ceptin' Sam on this occasion.'

'Including you?' asked Caleb.

'Yeh, including me,' replied the barber with a knowing smile. 'I'm just like the others. I'll attend meetin's, say my piece an' then wait for someone else to actually do somethin'. I don't mind admittin' it, Reverend, I'm a coward but it if means stayin' alive that's what I'll be. Besides, I'm over sixty, far too old to be a hero.'

Eventually Caleb climbed out of the tub, dried himself off with a large, rough towel and dressed. He then crossed the street to the hotel where he found a sour-looking man behind the desk. The man looked him up and down for a few moments and then sneered slightly.

'I guess you must be the preacher Luke was tellin' me about,' he said. 'I don't normally take blacks, Indians or mulattos. I still won't take Indians or mulattos but since you're a preacher I guess I can make an exception about not takin' blacks in your case.'

'Most kind of you,' said Caleb, sarcastically. The sarcasm appeared lost on the man. 'Mr Casey isn't it?' He extended his hand which the man took more out of surprise than anything else. 'I don't know how long I shall be here,' he continued. 'Perhaps I ought to pay for one week in advance.'

'A week!' muttered Casey. 'I don't know about that...'

'Are you expecting other guests?' asked Caleb. 'I understood this to be rather a slack time for you, especially since the cattle-drive ended a month ago.'

'Yeh, well,' muttered Casey, plainly ill at ease. 'OK, one week. Er ... did you say in advance?' He held out his hand. 'That'll be seven dollars. If you want food that's extra, dependin' on what you eat.'

Caleb smiled and took a ten-dollar bill from his wallet and handed it to Casey. 'Let's call it ten dollars including food,' he suggested. 'I'm an easy man to please, I don't expect anything fancy.'

'OK, ten dollars includin' food,' said Casey. 'It's just as well you don't expect no fancy cookin', especially some of that food I seen black folk eatin'.'

'Believe me,' said Caleb, grinning, 'I too have an aversion to that kind of food. Some people seem to think that because I am black I must like spicy food and plenty of rice. I can assure you that I am more at home with something like a large steak.'

'Good,' said Casey. 'There's three other guests stayin' at the moment. One is here to try an' sell the ranchers things to do with cattle, one is a gun salesman but I don't think he's havin' much luck sellin' any hardware in Beresford an' the other is a Miss Greaves. She's lived here for the last six years. She came into a load of money when

24

her brother died an' seems to like it here for some strange reason. Your room is at the back, first floor, number six.'

'Keeping me well out of sight,' said Caleb with a broad grin.

'Nope,' replied Casey, again missing the sarcasm. 'Front rooms are all let an' me an' Mrs Casey live on the top floor at the front.'

'The back will do just fine,' said Caleb. 'What time is the evening meal?'

'Six o'clock sharp,' said Casey. He indicated a door alongside the desk. 'Residents' lounge is through there an' I don't allow women in guest rooms. If you want that kind of thing there's some girls down at the saloon. Oh, an' just one more thing. I've just put a new carpet down in the lounge an' I'd appreciate it if you'd knock any mud off your boots before goin' in and, if you want a smoke, make sure the ash goes in the spittoons provided an' not on the carpet. Dinin'-room is through there…' He indicated a door opposite. 'Breakfast is seven o'clock sharp. If you want a drink you have to use the saloon. Are there any questions?'

'No, Mr Casey,' replied Caleb. 'I do believe you have covered everything. Room number six you said. I shall take my saddle and belongings up, I assume they will be

25

perfectly safe?'

'Your saddle will be,' said Casey. 'I wouldn't leave that rifle where it can be seen though. Sometimes folk leave their guns with Luke for safe keeping.'

'Then perhaps I will go and see him,' agreed Caleb. 'I thank you, Mr Casey. Until dinner time then.' He touched the brim of his hat, picked up his saddle and rifle and went upstairs.

The room turned out to be slightly larger than he had expected. In his experience rooms at the rear were usually quite small. He tested the bed, which seemed quite comfortable and examined it for bed-bugs. Bed-bugs, rooming-houses and a great many hotels seemed to go together and he was quite surprised when he did not discover any. In fact the general appearance of the hotel was that it was considerably cleaner than most. To his mind, a clean hotel probably meant good food and he was looking forward to his first decent meal in several weeks.

Before dinner he paid another visit to the sheriff's office where Luke Solomons agreed to look after his rifle. His Colts, he decided to keep with him. Without them he would feel naked and vulnerable.

TWO

At six o'clock sharp, having decided against wearing his guns to dinner, Caleb entered the dining-room where he discovered his fellow guests already at the single, large table. It was obvious that they had not been warned exactly who the extra guest was as all three looked at him with a mixture of horror and even fear. Miss Greaves, a woman who appeared to be in her late sixties, seemed particularly horrified. She self-consciously pulled a shawl across her chest and held it there.

'I think you must have the wrong room,' she said stiffly. 'This room is the dining-room and is for guests of the hotel.'

'Then I am in the right room,' said Caleb with a broad smile. 'Allow me to introduce myself. The Reverend Caleb Black, at your service.'

'Mr Casey said something about a minister taking a room,' muttered one of the two men. 'He did not say anything about you being a negro though.'

'Purely an oversight on his part I expect,' said Caleb, seating himself at the only vacant chair which happened to be next to Miss Greaves. 'I'm sure you'll agree that in the eyes of the Lord we are all the same colour.'

Miss Greaves was plainly ill at ease and pulled her shawl a little tighter.

'Perhaps in the eyes of the Lord ... er ... Reverend ... but I am not too certain about the law. It is my understanding that...'

'That negroes are inferior to white people?' said Caleb, smiling at her. 'Such a belief may well still prevail in some parts of the South but I seem to remember that there was a war quite recently which declared that all men, regardless of their race, creed or colour of skin, were equal. In fact I served as a lieutenant in the army on that basis. Perhaps I was mistaken, but I do not think so. I believe, since I was born a free man in the North and have served my country, I am entitled to the same rights and privileges as a white man.' Caleb was just warming to the subject he cared most about.

'Hell, Reverend,' interrupted the other man. 'Don't take it to heart so. Personally I don't give a damn what colour skin a man

28

has, he can't help that. It's just that it wasn't that long ago folk like you were slaves. It just takes a bit of getting used to, that's all. Don't you agree, Miss Greaves?'

'I'm sure I don't know what to make of it, Mr Waterman,' replied Miss Greaves stiffly. 'At least before the war people did have some sense of values. It is just a pity that good men such as my dear departed brother were forced to abandon all they held dear.' She turned and stared coldly at Caleb. 'He was an officer with the Confederate Army, a major in fact.'

'And I have no doubt that he was a good man,' said Caleb.

'Indeed he was, *Mr Black,*' she said between clenched teeth. 'A far better man than the likes of you will ever be.'

At that moment Ben Casey came into the room and obviously sensed the hostility. 'Ah, I see you have all met the Reverend Black,' he said, uneasily glancing at each of them in turn.

'Indeed we have, Mr Casey,' snorted Miss Greaves, standing up. 'I must ask you to serve my dinner in my room. I do not think I could eat in this atmosphere.' She stormed past Ben Casey and called back when she was through the door. 'It would appear that

I might have to reconsider my position here.' Ben Casey looked flustered and followed Miss Greaves, trying to placate her.

'Whoops!' said Waterman. 'Looks like Miss Greaves doesn't like you, Mr Black.'

'In that she is not alone,' muttered the other man, Horst Schultz. 'It is well that my business in Beresford is ended and I leave tomorrow.'

'I'm surprised you've stayed as long as you have, Mr Schultz,' said Waterman. 'You can't have sold many guns here.'

'They do not know a good gun when they see one,' grunted Schulz.

Mrs Casey entered the room carrying a tureen of soup which she placed in the centre of the table. She looked coldly at Caleb and then quite deliberately removed the place settings in front of him which she then placed on a tray.

'You'll have to eat in your room,' she snorted at him. 'I will not have my other guests upset by you, especially Miss Greaves. I would order you to leave at once but it is too late to expect you to find anywhere at this time of night. However, I must insist that you vacate your room immediately after breakfast. Your money will be refunded.'

'May I ask in exactly what way I have upset Miss Greaves?' asked Caleb.

'I told my husband he was making a big mistake in allowing a negro into the hotel,' she continued, ignoring Caleb's question. 'I told him exactly what the reaction would be from Miss Greaves.'

'I still do not understand why my presence should make Miss Greaves react as she did,' said Caleb.

'*Mr Black*,' she sighed. 'Miss Greaves has lived here a long time and I would like it to be a lot longer. Not that it is any business of yours, but she is from the South, I do not know exactly where from but I have become very friendly with her. I do know that she had a very unfortunate experience at the hands of some black men during the war. Sufficient to say that up to that point she had never known any man, black or white.'

'I see,' said Caleb. 'So one unfortunate experience means that all men of my colour are the same. Perhaps Mrs Boulton feels the same, even though her attackers included three white men.'

'Two,' corrected Mrs Casey. 'Young Jake Smith did not do anything. I'm sorry, Mr Black, but I must ask you to vacate your room in the morning. There is nothing more to say on the matter. I shall take your meal up to your room.' Caleb shrugged and chose not to pursue the matter.

Although the confrontation had dented Caleb's appetite somewhat, he still enjoyed his dinner of roast beef. After he had eaten he sat for some time staring out of the window, which overlooked the back yard, considered his position and studied the Wanted posters.

The first was for $750 for Courtney Williams, also known as Black Bill, wanted for robbery, rape and assault. The second showed a picture of someone who was plainly an Indian but which seemed to owe more to the work of an artist's imagination than a true likeness. Known only as 'Sioux', he was also wanted for robbery, rape and assault and offered a reward of $500. Next came the picture of a white man with a livid scar down his left cheek by the name of James Hooper, also known as Hoppy. He had a reward of $200. A man named as Saul Green who, the poster claimed, had vivid ginger hair, was worth $100. Both Hooper and Green were wanted for robbery and assault. Finally came Jake Smith, $50, whose only crime appeared to be one known robbery.

The total of $1,600 was not among the most valuable of rewards Caleb had gone after, but he hardly ever refused even a single reward of fifty dollars if it came his way. Now, he wondered if it was worth his while.

After about ten minutes there was a knock on his door and Sheriff Luke Solomons came in. He sat on the bed and looked at Caleb rather sadly.

'Sorry things didn't work out, Reverend,' he eventually said. 'I forgot all about Miss Greaves.'

'You can't be held to blame,' said Caleb. 'These things happen. I have found, from experience, that it is invariably women like Miss Greaves who hold extreme views and not always Southern women. Is there anywhere else in town I can stay?'

'No, 'fraid not,' said the sheriff. 'There is a place what opens up as a roomin' house durin' the cattle drive and I have asked if you can stay there. They just don't want to know.'

'Then it looks like I shall have to forget about going after Black Bill,' said Caleb. 'Ah well, that is life I suppose.'

'Yeh, pity though,' said the sheriff. 'I had this feelin' that you might've been able to get the better of Black Bill. I have talked to Miss Greaves but she won't change her mind. I didn't say nothin' about you bein' a bounty hunter. Come on along to the saloon. I'll buy you a drink, it's the least I can do.'

'And earn yourself a reputation as a lover of blacks,' said Caleb.

'Don't you worry none about my reputation,' said the sheriff. 'If folk don't like it they can always vote me out of office an' I won't lose no sleep over that. Anyhow, I don't think that'll happen. They know there ain't nobody fool enough to take the job, especially at the salary they pay.'

'Very well, Sheriff,' said Caleb. 'You can buy me a drink. I trust that there will be no objections or there is some obscure law which says that negroes cannot be served?'

'None,' replied the sheriff. 'I know Tom Gittins – he owns the saloon – don't give a shit what colour a man's skin is as long as he pays for his drinks. The law in this state says that no Indians or mulattos can be served, but it don't say nothin' about negroes.'

The saloon was reasonably full but a deathly silence descended as Caleb and the sheriff entered. It was not until the pair reached the bar that people started to talk amongst themselves and it was obvious just who was the main topic of conversation. The bartender, obviously not Tom Gittins, appeared rather reluctant to serve Caleb and it was not until Tom Gittins appeared and took over that a beer was placed in front of Caleb. Immediately everyone started talking at once and, very slowly, an air of normality returned.

'Everyone's heard all about what happened between you an' Miss Greaves at the hotel,' said Gittins. 'Pity that, you bein' a preacher as well. Still, there's no accountin' for how folk behave. Mind, she is from the South so I guess that explains a lot. The word is that she was raped by some black men down there.'

'So I believe,' said Caleb. 'I am not a Southerner though. How do the others feel about it?'

'Some say it's no more than somebody like you deserves but most don't seem bothered either way,' said Gittins. 'As for me, you pay your way an' you can drink all you like.'

Luke Solomons looked round the room and seemed satisfied that everything had returned to normal, apart from Sam Boulton who sat morosely in a corner, staring at them with obvious hatred. When he saw Luke watching him he drained his glass and clattered from the room, making loud comments about being particular where he drank, who he drank with and inviting others to join him. None did.

'Tom,' said Luke to Tom Gittins, 'can we talk in your office?'

'Sure,' replied Tom. 'Give me a couple of minutes. You can go through.'

Luke nudged Caleb, indicating that he should follow him and, when Tom Gittins arrived, Luke checked that nobody was about.

'Reverend,' he said to Caleb. 'Tom here is a member of the town council and just about the only man I can trust. I want him to know exactly what you do for a livin', if that's OK with you?'

'I suppose it will have to come out some time,' replied Caleb. 'Be my guest, Sheriff.'

'Bounty hunter!' said Gittins when the sheriff had explained. 'I can't say as I hold much with bounty hunters, but each to his own, I suppose. I've got to admit though that we need to do somethin' about Black Bill so I guess someone like you is the best man for the job.'

'There's just the problem of him havin' somewhere to stay,' said the sheriff. 'Ida

36

Casey won't have him at the hotel at any price. I also talked to Mr Wilberforce but he claimed that he doesn't have any room for a guest. That's a load of bull of course, there's three bedrooms at his place and only him an' his wife. I wondered if you had a spare room.'

Tom Gittins looked at both men for a moment and then smiled. 'Well, everybody knows I've got five rooms used by my girls. I suppose you could share with one of them if the fancy takes you, Reverend.' He laughed and shook his head. 'No, I guess not, you bein' a minister of religion an' all that. Anyhow, I make it a rule that my girls are not allowed to entertain a client all night so I guess I can't make an exception even for a reverend. OK, I'll tell you what, Reverend. I've got a small room next to this office I sometimes use as a store room. It isn't anything grand but at least it's dry. I'll have it cleaned out and a bed put in if you like.'

'That sounds fine,' said Caleb. 'When can I move in? I don't want to outstay my welcome at the hotel. Mrs Casey was gracious enough to allow me to remain there until tomorrow morning, but I don't think she would lose any sleep if I moved out tonight.'

'Come back in a couple of hours,' said Gittins. 'The bed won't be as comfortable as the one at the hotel but it's better than nothin'. I can also guarantee there won't be no bed-bugs – I've banned 'em!' He laughed drily. 'Leastways my wife has banned 'em an' nobody an' nothin' argues with her.'

'Then perhaps you had better check that she is agreeable to my staying here,' suggested Caleb. 'I would hate to come between man and wife.'

'She'll be fine,' promised Gittins. 'Still, if it bothers you, you can check with her yourself. I'll go get her.' Without waiting for a reply, Tom Gittins left the room and returned a few minutes later with a large, well-dressed woman who looked at Caleb a little coldly.

'I saw you ride into town,' she said. 'I remember thinking that you were different from most other black men I've seen. Oh, I've met quite a few in my time and I have to say that I was never very impressed by any of them. I thought that you looked like a man who knew his own mind and obviously took care with his appearance. That's something a great many white men could do with learning about as well. Very well, I have no objection. Of course we run a business here and are not in the habit of giving charity. The charge is five dollars a week, including food. You eat the same as my girls. Nothing fancy, just good, plain cooking.'

'You have just found yourself another customer,' agreed Caleb. 'I shall return in about two hours with my belongings, such as they are.'

'Just one thing,' said Mrs Gittins. 'This is what some of your kind, Mr Wilberforce among them, call a house of ill repute. That's not what I call it, I call it a business, a very good business. Folk come here to drink, gamble and make use of my girls. If they want religion they go down the street to the church and Mr Wilberforce. I don't perform any church services and don't expect Mr Wilberforce to supply beer, gaming tables or girls. I do not want you going round preaching the evils of drink, gambling or women to my customers or girls. Do you understand?'

'You make yourself very plain, Mrs Gittins,' said Caleb with a broad grin. 'It is a deal. Do not worry about me. I am not one of those self-righteous ministers who claim that such things are sinful. Indeed, I have been known to play the occasional game of cards myself and I certainly enjoy a drink.'

'Then I guess we'll get along just fine,' said Mrs Gittins. 'I take it that you have already eaten?' Caleb nodded. 'Good,' she continued. 'We don't get up as early as some and breakfast is normally about nine o'clock. Is there anything you don't eat?'

'You put it in front of me, Mrs Gittins, and I'll eat it,' said Caleb.

Luke Solomons left Caleb in the bar, saying that he had work to do but would be back later. Caleb ordered another beer and sat himself at an empty table, the one previously occupied by Sam Boulton. There were a few comments from other customers, which he ignored, but most appeared concerned with more important matters such as drinking and playing cards. A few played blackjack or roulette and there seemed to be a steady flow of other customers up the stairs in company of one bar-girl or other. It was noticeable that none of the girls approached Caleb to offer their services. Whether this was because he was a preacher or because he was black, he neither knew nor cared.

He eventually returned to the hotel and collected his belongings. On the way downstairs he was met by Ida Casey who seemed quite surprised to see him.

'I have been offered a room in the saloon,' explained Caleb. 'Perhaps it is as well, I do not wish to cause you any trouble.'

'At least Miss Greaves will be pleased,' replied Mrs Casey, tartly. 'I hope you don't think it was me who had anything to do with it, Mr Black. I can assure you that had it not been for Miss Greaves I would not have said anything. If you wait a minute I'll get you your money. There will be a charge of one dollar for the meal though.'

'And a very good meal it was,' said Caleb. 'It is a pity Miss Greaves reacted so badly and I appreciate that you do have to put the considerations of your regular customers first. Please tender my apologies to Miss Greaves for any distress I may have caused her and you can assure her that not all black men are out to assault white women.'

'I'll tell her,' said Mrs Casey. 'Not that it will do any good.' She disappeared into a side room and returned a short time later with Caleb's money.

There was considerable interest when Caleb walked through the saloon carrying his saddle and rifle and even louder comments when he went into his room. As promised, a bed had been installed, along with a small dressing-table, bowl and jug of water. The bed seemed comfortable enough, although not as comfortable as the one in the hotel, but after sleeping rough for many days, any bed was welcome. Out of pure habit he examined the bed for unwelcoming visitors but did not find any.

Having heard the comments from a small but very vocal element of the customers in the bar, Caleb felt it prudent to wear his guns. He had found from long experience that drink and such people often led to some form of confrontation and he liked to be prepared. He had noticed that very few customers wore guns and this was quite normal but he had also found that most carried knives of some kind and were often prepared to use them. He also remembered the threat made by Sam Boulton, although he suspected that it was mainly talk on his part. However, there was always at least one person who tried to egg on people like Boulton. As ever, his guns were hidden under his long coat and it seemed that nobody noticed them.

He was about to order a beer when Luke Solomons arrived looking somewhat agitated. He ordered two beers and waited for the sheriff to say something.

'I've just heard that Black Bill is somewhere about,' he said. 'One of the farmers reckons he saw three of his men down by the river, the half-breed an' two whites.'

'Is that unusual?' asked Caleb.

'At this time of night, yes,' said Luke. 'It looks like they're plannin' somethin' but what or when is anybody's guess.'

'Down by the river?' said Caleb. 'Is that far from town?'

'About a mile,' said Luke. 'The farmer said that they were this side of the river, which means they probably crossed by the bridge a couple of miles further up.'

'Can this farmer be relied upon?' queried Caleb. 'Is it not possible that the three people he saw were either from Beresford or perhaps youngsters?'

'It's possible I suppose,' admitted Luke, 'but Mick Glasson farms along that part of the river and he knows most folk and the youngsters in town. Anyhow, they had horses with them and if youngsters go out there they don't take horses. No, he was quite certain it was the half-breed, Hoppy Hooper and Saul Green. He was worried enough to move his wife and family out of their farm and bring them into town. Now he's worried about them wreckin' his farm.'

'Then, Sheriff,' said Caleb. 'I have a suggestion. We both ride out there and see if we can capture them.'

'In the dark?' exclaimed Luke.

'Yes, Sheriff,' said Caleb. 'In the dark. They will not be expecting us.'

'Hell, Reverend,' complained the sheriff. 'My eyes ain't none too good in daylight, let alone in the dark.' He looked at Caleb and smiled. 'It's OK for you. You bein' the colour you are you'll just blend in.'

'Being black does have a few advantages,' said Caleb, also smiling. 'However, since I am the one who is out to earn money by the arrest of these men, perhaps I should not expect you to risk your neck. Just point me in the right direction and I will do the rest.'

'And have everybody say that I was shit scared of the dark?' said Luke. 'No, sir. OK, we both go. Anyhow, tryin' to describe how to get there might be easy enough but in the dark is a different thing. I'll meet you down by the livery in ten minutes. Oh, an' if I was you I'd go out by the back door so's nobody sees you.'

'And why shouldn't anyone see me?' asked Caleb.

'Because I think somebody in town tells Black Bill everythin' that's goin' on,' replied the sheriff. 'I don't know who, but one day

I'll find out. The chances are he already knows about you.'

'They would have to move pretty fast to get a message out to him, especially at this time of night,' said Caleb.

'Maybe so,' agreed the sheriff. 'The other reason is that they're a nosy lot round here an' if they see you goin' out with your saddle somebody is sure to follow an' the last thing I want is havin' to protect anyone.'

'Won't the farmer have told others?' asked Caleb.

'No, I told him to keep quiet. Him and his family have checked into the hotel and I've made Ben and Ida Casey swear they'll say nothin' for the moment. If word gets about it might cause a bit of a panic.'

'Very well,' agreed Caleb. 'The livery in ten minutes.'

THREE

In order not to attract any attention, Caleb and his saddle left the room through the window and then he went down to the livery along the rear of the buildings. It was only

45

when he had to cross the street to the livery that he was open to prying eyes. He waited a few minutes for a solitary figure to get well out of the way before crossing. He found Luke Solomons waiting for him. Ten minutes later they were on their way.

'Maybe it was as well you came along,' observed Caleb. 'I don't think I'd ever have found the place in the dark.'

'Bein' dark can work both for and against us,' said Luke. 'At least they won't be expectin' us. Against that is the fact that we might easily lose them.'

'Always assuming they are still there,' said Caleb. 'As it is we don't know exactly where they are or even if it was three of Black Bill's men. We've only got that farmer's word for it and it was dark when he saw them. Even if it was them, we might never find them, they might have moved on or they might only be a few feet away and we'll walk past them.'

'That's a chance we'll have to take,' said Luke. 'Mick Glasson don't make mistakes, he saw them, I'm certain of that.'

Twenty minutes later, they reached the bridge and turned downstream and followed the river easily enough, if very slowly, for at least another half-hour before Luke called a halt. They found a few bushes where they hitched their horses.

'Mick Glasson said they were about a couple of miles down from the bridge an' I reckon this is about as far as we can go without bein' seen or heard,' said Luke. 'There's a clump of trees about two hundred yards down there so that's more'n like where they are if they've stayed for some reason. I just wish I knew what the hell they're doin' here.'

'If we find them, perhaps we'll find out,' said Caleb. 'Lead the way, Sheriff. I don't think rifles will be much use, this is going to be close-quarter work and they will probably only get in the way. I'll leave mine here. It's too dark to use them even if they do manage to make a run for it.'

'Yeh, I reckon you're right,' agreed the sheriff. 'Keep as quiet as you can. I hear that Sioux can hear a fly buzzin' round a piece of shit at a hundred yards. That's probably all talk but we can't take the chance.'

'I can be as quiet as the grave if need be,' assured Caleb.

A distance of 200 yards in daylight was not very far, but that same distance in almost total darkness made it seem a very long way, not helped by the fact that they had to avoid anything underfoot which might alert their quarry. After a time, Luke gripped Caleb's arm and nodded ahead.

It was just possible to make out a line of trees and both men crouched, listened and waited for some considerable time. Eventually, Caleb took the initiative and indicated that the sheriff should follow the river bank while he circled round. The sheriff nodded his agreement and disappeared into the darkness.

Finding his way round was not easy but Caleb's eyesight was very good and he managed to keep the trees in view against the dim skyline. At first there was no indication that the outlaws were there. There was no fire, no sound of talking and not even the sounds made by someone asleep. In fact the only sound was the faint noise made by the river.

Quite suddenly, Caleb found himself amongst the trees, almost walking into one of them. Once again he stopped and listened but could not hear anything. In fact he was on the point of admitting that he and Luke were probably wasting their time and that the three men had moved on or had never been there. However he knew they had to make certain. He moved further among the trees, both guns at the ready, cautiously feeling his way with his feet and drawing back a few times as he felt something under his feet. Suddenly he froze.

Somewhere ahead, not too far, he heard the distinct sound of someone snoring. It was very brief and the snort was suddenly choked to be followed by a muttered curse. He instinctively breathed a sigh of relief, pleased that they were not wasting their time.

The problem now was to discover exactly where the outlaws were and then to get close enough to take them by surprise. He wondered where the sheriff was at that moment. That, however, was something he could not know. To all intents and purposes he was on his own. The snoring started again to be quickly followed by somebody else swearing quietly at the offender. There was an answering mutter and the snoring stopped.

He slowly and quietly moved forward a few yards, stopped and listened. The sound of breathing could now be plainly heard and he guessed that he was no more than a few feet from them. From that point onwards it was a matter of inching his way forward, listening intently and straining his eyes. The last thing he wanted to do was trip over any of them.

How he missed it he would never know, but Caleb suddenly found himself walking into the side of horse. The horse snorted and bucked slightly and Caleb found himself stroking the horse's muzzle to quieten it. It seemed to work.

His eyes had grown accustomed to the darkness a long time before, but even so, in the absence of any moonlight, it was very difficult to see anything. He did find the other two horses and stroked them to assure them. He then sank to one knee and studied the ground in front of him but he was unable to make out anything definite. The movement of someone turning under what was probably a blanket finally established where the three men were.

Caleb was just about to move forward when he suddenly became aware of someone very close by. His grip tightened on his guns just in case it turned out not to be the sheriff. A figure suddenly loomed alongside and Caleb instinctively grasped the sheriff's arm. It was obvious that the sheriff had not seen him and Caleb suddenly felt the barrel of a gun being pressed against his head.

'It's me!' hissed Caleb. The sheriff grunted and lowered his gun. Caleb pointed in the direction of the three sleeping forms hoping that the sheriff could also see them and nodded the sheriff forward. Whether or not the sheriff saw the nod he did not know, but they both moved forward.

The sheriff went to the nearest form and Caleb to the one furthest away, leaving the third man between them. They pulled the blankets off of the two men and held their guns against their heads.

'What the hell's goin' on?' demanded the man the sheriff had uncovered. Caleb had immediately taken the precaution of clamping his hand across the mouth of his target. The figure in the middle suddenly sat up.

'Just take it easy,' warned the sheriff. 'It might be dark but you're close enough for us not to miss.'

'Take their guns,' said Caleb. 'You,' he ordered the man between them, 'hand over your gun and make it very slow. Don't think I won't shoot. I will. Now, do as you are told, hand over your gun.'

'Who the hell are you an' what the hell do you want?' demanded one of the men.

'Sheriff Luke Solomons,' said the sheriff. 'You are all under arrest.'

The man between them slowly rose to his feet and apparently went through the motions of removing his gun. He was removing his gun but, as Caleb soon discovered, not with any intention of handing it over.

There were two shots, the first fired by the outlaw, the second fired by Caleb. Caleb felt a sharp twinge and knew that he had been hit in his right, upper arm, though obviously not seriously. Whether or not his bullet had struck home he did not find out. The figure suddenly leapt over the body of the man held by the sheriff and was immediately lost in the blackness. There was no time for either Caleb or the sheriff to react and the man managed to get to the horses and take one. The horse could be heard crashing through the bushes but there was nothing to be done to stop him.

'Ah well, at least we got two of them,' said Caleb, removing the gun from his man. 'Now, take it very slowly. Stand up.'

'I don't know what the hell you think you is playin' at, Sheriff,' hissed the man held by the sheriff, 'but that was Sioux who got away. Black Bill will know all about this before it gets light.'

'Then we'll be waiting for him,' said Caleb.

'An' just who the hell are you?' demanded the other man.

'Caleb Black, the Reverend Caleb Black,' replied Caleb. 'Don't let the title fool you, I make it my business to save the souls of people like you and earn some money from the rewards out on them.'

'Bounty hunter!' snarled the man. 'Yeh, it makes sense, the sheriff here wouldn't have the guts to do anythin' like this on his own.' He peered closely at Caleb. 'Hey, you look like a negro.'

'And the sheriff was quite certain that nobody would be able to tell in the dark,' laughed Caleb. 'Indeed I am. Black by name and black by colour.'

'Then I'd make sure I got my money an' then got the hell out of it as soon as I could, Mr Bounty Hunter,' said the man. 'When Black Bill hears about this we won't be in jail for five minutes after he hits town. You ought to know what'll happen, Sheriff. I reckon that pretty soon Beresford will be lookin' for a new sheriff.'

'Just shut up an' move,' ordered the sheriff. 'Don't get any ideas about makin' a run for it either, a bullet don't need daylight to hit its target.'

'What about our horses?' demanded the other man.

'You can walk,' said Caleb. 'They'll be safe

enough here until the morning. Now do as the man says, start walking and, remember, we are right behind you.'

It took about twenty minutes to reach the two horses tethered by Caleb and the sheriff and, surprisingly as far as Caleb was concerned, neither man made any attempt to make a break for it. When they did find their horses, Caleb took some twine from his saddle-bag and tied the hands of the two outlaws behind them. The two men seemed to think it funny and made constant wisecracks. An hour later they were being locked in the jail.

'Hoppy Hooper an' Saul Green,' said the sheriff. 'I guess that means you just earned yourself three hundred dollars. Not a bad night's work.'

'I wouldn't have been able to manage it on my own,' said Caleb, stripping off his jacket and examining his wound. 'I'd say that entitles you to half of it.' He peered closely at his arm and grunted. 'Just a scratch, I'll survive.'

The sheriff laughed drily. 'They don't pay rewards to lawmen in this state,' he said. 'They reckon ten dollars a week is reward enough.'

'Probably so,' agreed Caleb, replacing his

jacket. 'I don't think there is any law against someone like me showing my appreciation though.'

'No, I guess not,' said the sheriff. 'It wouldn't do to broadcast it though.'

'If you don't tell anyone, neither will I,' said Caleb. 'As you say, a half-share in three hundred isn't bad for a few hours' work, but I'd rather be handing a half-share in sixteen hundred over to you.'

'You know,' said the sheriff. 'I've met a couple of bounty hunters before and I even helped them to catch outlaws, but you're the first one who has said he'll share the reward. There's a big difference between sixteen hundred and eight hundred.'

'And there's a bigger difference between eight hundred and nothing,' said Caleb. 'I don't mind, I'm not a greedy man. In fact I've ended up giving most of my rewards away to good causes in the past. Just so long as I have enough money in my pocket to get by, that's fine by me.'

'Well, I'll put it this way,' said the sheriff. 'If I happen to find whatever you think fit suddenly appearing in my hand, I won't argue.'

'Then it's settled,' said Caleb. 'What about Black Bill, do you think he'll come and try to rescue them?'

'Nothin' more certain,' said Luke. 'He thinks he's got this territory all to himself and he won't like it when somebody else moves in to challenge him, for whatever reason.'

'I've heard that before,' said Caleb. 'For the most part though they've thought about their own skins and left folk like these two to take their chances with the law. Why should Black Bill be any different?'

'You could be right, I suppose,' said Luke. 'Somehow though, I don't think we've seen the last of him. Be ready for trouble in the mornin'. I don't think anythin' will happen tonight.'

'I think someone ought to stay here and keep watch though,' said Caleb. 'I'll make myself comfortable if you like, you get along home to your wife, she'll be worrying about you.'

'And you're goin' to need some sleep as well,' said Luke. 'I'll get Ted in, he ain't got no family to worry about.'

There was a knock on the door and both men immediately drew their guns. Luke slowly pulled back the corner of a blind and peered out.

'Tom Gittins,' he said. 'What the hell does

he want at this time of night?'

'I suggest you let him in and find out,' said Caleb. Luke opened the door.

'What the hell's goin' on?' demanded the saloon-owner when he came in. 'I just heard that you came into town with two prisoners.'

'And who told you that?' asked Luke. 'We didn't see nobody.'

'But somebody saw you,' said Tom. 'I also knew somethin' was afoot earlier on when I saw the preacher's room was empty.'

'I should've known it'd be impossible to keep somethin' like this quiet,' said Luke. 'There's nothin' can happen in this town without somebody seein' it.'

'Better than the telegraph,' said Tom. 'I think you owe somebody an explanation.'

'We've got Hoppy Hooper and Saul Green,' said the sheriff, with a resigned sigh. 'Didn't your informant know who it was?'

'All he saw was you bringing two men in,' said Tom. 'Hooper and Green! I hope you know what you're doin' Luke. What happens when Black Bill finds out? It can only mean trouble.'

'Perhaps I was mistaken,' said Caleb. 'But I seem to remember you saying that something needed to be done. Well, the sheriff and me have done something.'

'Yeh, well,' faltered Tom. 'I agree that somethin' needs doin' but I wasn't expecting anything to happen quite so soon. One thing's for certain, the whole town is goin' to know about it at first light, if they don't know already.'

'And they ought to be pleased,' said Caleb.

'The only time they'll be pleased is when they see Black Bill and his men swingin' on the end of a rope,' said Tom. 'In the meantime most of them will be shittin' their pants wonderin' what's goin' to happen.'

'I wasn't aware that they had committed any hanging offences,' said Caleb.

'You know what I mean,' snapped the saloon-owner. 'I can assure you that if there is any trouble and particularly if anyone gets killed, you'll be held to blame.'

'And not helped by the fact that I, like Black Bill, am also black,' said Caleb. 'I could, of course, quite easily simply walk away from it all. If you want to get rid of this man and his men then you have to make a stand sometime. The choice is yours, Mr Gittins.'

Before Tom Gittins could reply there was another urgent hammering on the door followed by demands to be allowed in. Luke opened the door and immediately several people burst in, Sam Boulton in the lead. They were closely followed by the deputy sheriff.

'I tried talkin' them out of this,' gasped the deputy, 'but they wouldn't listen. They heard somethin' about you havin' two of Black Bill's men locked up.'

'That's what we heard, Sheriff,' growled Sam Boulton. 'Is it true?'

'It is,' replied Luke. 'The reverend an' me arrested them a couple of hours ago out at Mick Glasson's place.'

'Mick Glasson!' said Boulton. 'Are they all right?'

'Safe an' well,' said the sheriff. 'They came into town earlier on an' told me where three of Black Bill's men were. They checked into the hotel.'

'Three?' queried Boulton. 'What happened to the other one?'

'Unfortunately he got away,' said Caleb.

'An' just how do you fit into all this, *Reverend?*' demanded Boulton.

'I think that perhaps an explanation is in order,' said Caleb. 'I am indeed a minister of the church, but I also supplement my income by bringing men such as Black Bill to justice.'

'A bounty hunter!' snarled Boulton. 'Now I heard everythin'. Don't you realize just what you've done, *Mr Bounty Hunter?* Black Bill will take his revenge on this town. It's all very well for you, you don't live here, we do.'

'Yeh,' said one of the others. 'I say them two go free now, before Black Bill gets here.'

'Free!' exclaimed Luke. 'Is that what you really want? Ever since he turned up most of you have been complainin' that somebody ought to do somethin' about Black Bill. Now somebody does somethin' you want to turn 'em free. I don't understand you at all. You least of all, Sam. Your wife was raped by those men, remember, or have you forgotten?'

'I ain't forgotten, Sheriff,' snarled Sam Boulton. 'Just the opposite. I don't want 'em doin' the same thing again. I say them two go free – now.'

'The only way they'll go free is if you kill me first,' said Luke, squaring up at the door through to the cells.

'I suppose that means you'll also have to kill me,' said Caleb, joining him.

'Killin' you would be a pleasure,' snarled Boulton.

'Because a black man raped your wife?' said Caleb. 'There were also a couple of white men from what I hear. I suppose it's all right for a white man to rape a white woman but not a black man or a half-breed.'

'It doesn't matter to me what colour they were,' a woman's voice suddenly said. Mrs Boulton pushed her way forward. 'Black, white or Indian, rape is still rape.' She stared angrily at her husband. 'I'm ashamed of you, Sam Boulton,' she continued. 'At last somebody has the guts to do something about Black Bill and his men and all you want to do is let them go. Well I for one am right behind the reverend and the sheriff and I suspect that every other woman in town is as well.'

'You don't know what you're talkin' about, woman,' snarled Sam. 'Black Bill ain't goin' to take this lyin' down.'

'But you expect a woman to take it lying down – literally,' she sneered. 'I think you'll find that all the women of Beresford are right behind you, Sheriff.' Two other women pushed past and announced their agreement with Mrs Boulton. The arrival of several more women obviously made the men think again.

'OK, folk,' said the sheriff. 'The party's over. Now you all know what's happened. I agree that Black Bill is not goin' to stand by an' do nothin' but I don't think it'll happen tonight. I suggest you all go back home and be ready for him when it gets light.'

'You expect us to stand an' fight him!' exclaimed one of the other men. 'Hell, Luke, agreein' that you did the right thing is one thing but expectin' us to risk our lives is another. We ain't gunmen, in fact most of us don't even have decent guns an' I doubt if any of us could actually shoot a man, outlaw or not. That's your job, it's what you're paid for.'

'Yes, Aaron,' said the sheriff with a re-signed sigh. 'That's what I'm paid for, such as it is. OK, folks, get back to your homes an' let me an' the reverend get some sleep. We need to be wide awake when he does come.'

The women in the group grabbed hold of their men and guided them out of the office. Those men who were not being escorted by their wives made mutterings about the trouble that was to come, but they too vacated the office. When they had all gone Luke opened a drawer and took out a bottle of whisky and three glasses. He poured a measure each for himself, Caleb and Ted.

'It would appear that we have stirred up something of a hornets' nest,' observed

62

Caleb, sipping his whisky. 'Do you think the men will listen to their wives?'

'Most will do what they're told,' said Luke. 'I wouldn't like to rely on any of them to stand up to Black Bill though.' He drained his glass and poured out another good measure. He offered the bottle to Caleb who refused. 'Ted, I want you to stay here tonight,' continued Luke. 'Me an' the reverend need some sleep. You call me straight away if there's the slightest hint of trouble.'

'Yes, sir,' said Ted. 'Like you though, I don't think Black Bill will be here too early. Don't you worry none, I'll be OK.'

'Well I've had enough excitement for one night,' said Luke. 'You'd better get back to the saloon, Reverend. Tom might lock up on you. I'll see you later.'

Caleb returned to the saloon, where he found Tom Gittins waiting for him. He was offered another drink, which he refused. 'I don't mind admittin' that I'm shit scared,' said Tom. 'I know I said somethin' needed doin' but I didn't expect it to happen quite so soon.'

'It was necessary to act when we did,' said Caleb. 'If nothing else it might force Black Bill into the open.'

'That's what scares me,' said Tom. 'As far as I know he hasn't murdered anyone yet, but I don't want to be the first.'

'Support your sheriff and there won't be any need for anyone to be killed,' said Caleb. 'In my experience men like Black Bill back down very quickly when they are faced with a united opposition.'

'You saw 'em,' muttered Tom. 'I'd hardly call it united opposition.'

'Then it falls to me, the sheriff, Ted and possibly you,' said Caleb. 'That's four against three. I'll take those odds any time. Now, I must get some sleep. I have the feeling that it's going to be a long day tomorrow.'

FOUR

Caleb was up early, just as dawn broke, having had only four hours of sleep, but he was used to that and rarely needed more than six hours under normal circumstances. There was no sign of life in the saloon and he quietly let himself out through the back door. The street seemed unnaturally quiet and deserted and Caleb did not believe it was because the populace were late risers. People were plainly keeping themselves indoors in anticipation of what was to come. Sheriff Luke Solomons appeared at his office at the same time as Caleb.

'It looks like most folk have decided to lie in this mornin',' observed Luke.

'Are you surprised?' asked Caleb. 'I certainly am not. I have the feeling that the three of us are on our own. Perhaps Tom Gittins will join us but somehow I don't think he will. I take it that there is nobody else you can call on?'

'It's always the same,' said Luke, shaking his head. 'They're always ready to shout loud enough about somethin' needin' to be done, but you saw how they were last night, when somethin' is done, they just don't want to get involved. Ah well, maybe it's a good thing, most of 'em would only get in the way.'

'Perhaps you are right,' said Caleb. 'As one of them remarked, they are not gunfighters and as you probably know yourself, it is not easy to shoot to kill a man, although it does, unfortunately, become easier after the first time. I know my first time was hard and even now I find it difficult to kill in cold blood.'

'So they tell me,' said Luke. 'I've been a sheriff for almost twenty years now and I've never had to shoot a man yet, but that don't mean I wouldn't if I had to. The same applies to them.'

'What are you going to do about their horses and saddles?' asked Caleb. 'Somebody ought to go out there and bring them in. It shouldn't take too long.'

'They can wait,' said Luke. 'They won't go far. Anyhow, I don't think we'd get any volunteers and you, me and Ted will be needed here. We'd be accused of runnin' scared if Black Bill was to turn up when we weren't here.'

'When do you expect Black Bill?' asked Caleb.

The sheriff shrugged. 'Who can tell? He could arrive in the next ten minutes or it might be later on tonight when it gets dark. Whenever it is, we need to be ready. It all depends on how close he was to town.'

'Have you asked them what they were doing down by the river yet?'

'No, I couldn't be bothered last night,' replied the sheriff. 'I don't think we would've got a sensible answer then and I don't think we'll get a sensible answer now. Come on inside, we can both ask them.'

Caleb followed the sheriff into the office where they found Ted in the process of cooking himself and the prisoners a breakfast of ham and eggs.

'They get to eat better'n most folk,' observed Ted. 'There's coffee in the pot if you want it.' Caleb and the sheriff both nodded and helped themselves. 'They didn't lose no sleep last night,' continued Ted. 'In fact one of 'em kept me awake most of the night with his snorin'. Then this mornin' they seemed to think that it was only a matter of a couple of hours before Black Bill set 'em free.'

'It would appear that most of the townsfolk have the same idea,' said Caleb. 'Normally, most towns are quite busy at this time of the morning but I saw only two people, both of them opening up their stores.'

'An' I reckon that's how it'll stay for most of the day,' said Luke. 'Let's go talk to 'em. Don't expect no proper answers though.'

'There is just one thing,' said Ted. 'I did overhear one of 'em sayin' somethin' about the mornin' stage.'

'I'd forgotten all about that,' said Luke. 'We get the stagecoach twice a week, once in each direction. I wouldn't have thought there would be that much on it to interest them though. They have robbed it three times before, but apart from the mail and whatever the passengers are carryin', there's nothin' much on it.'

'There is that gun salesman, Horst Schultz, I think his name is,' said Caleb. 'He said that he was leaving today. Perhaps they want the guns he's carrying. I have no idea how many he's got.'

'I shouldn't think he's the target,' said Luke. 'All he's got is a case of samples, maybe six guns in all. No, if they were after the stage it was probably just to show that they were still around. They have been a bit quiet of late. They haven't even bothered with the mail the other times.'

'Perhaps they can't read,' suggested Caleb, wryly.

'Who knows?' said Luke. 'Anyhow, let's ask 'em.'

As expected, Hooper and Green were very uncooperative, claiming that they had made camp by the river simply because they were late and it was too far to travel back to their hideout.

Saul Green looked at Caleb, and sneered. 'You dress real fancy for a negro,' he said. 'In fact if'n I didn't know better I'd say you

68

was a preacher just like you said you was last night, but I didn't buy that then an' I don't now. Yeh, most preachers I ever met dress just like you. I guess you bein' a black man lets you out though.'

'Why?' asked Caleb. 'Don't negroes believe in God?'

'Yeh, I guess they do,' said Green. 'But I ain't never met a black what can even read or write before though an' to be a preacher you have to know how to read the Bible at least. It's full of real big words, most of which don't seem to have much meanin' 'ceptin' to a preacher.'

'Can you read and write?' asked Caleb.

'I can write my name,' replied Green, somewhat proudly. 'That's more'n Black Bill an' Hoppy here can do.'

'Yeh,' said Hooper. 'I can count up to one hundred though, which is more'n you can.'

'Well I *am* a minister of the church,' said Caleb. 'As you see I am also a negro and I can, I assure you, read all the big words in the Bible and even know what they mean. Now, I do not believe that you were out by the river simply because you were late. I think you were going to attack the Glasson farm. Why?'

'Think what you like, Mr Preacherman,'

sneered Hoppy Hooper. 'When Black Bill gets here you'll wish it was only the farm we attacked.'

'Ted overheard you talkin' about the stage,' said Luke. 'Were you plannin' to attack it? I wouldn't have thought there was that much on it to interest you, as you must have found out by now.'

'Maybe,' said Green, with a broad grin. 'Maybe we was, maybe we wasn't. You'll never know for sure. Maybe even we was plannin' to set fire to this whole damned town an' kill everybody in it.'

Ted brought in the ham and eggs for the prisoners and the sheriff decided that he was wasting his time and nodded for Caleb to follow him. The two men sat with mugs of hot coffee in their hands for some time before the door opened and a tall, very thin man entered, dressed very much like Caleb. He stared at Caleb with some obvious hostility for a short time.

'Have you seen enough?' asked Caleb. 'Yes, Mr Wilberforce – I take it you are the Reverend Wilberforce – I am indeed black and I am indeed also a minister.'

'And, from what I hear, well able and ready to use that gun you wear,' snorted Wilberforce. 'That is hardly an ability suited to a man of your apparent calling.'

'Each to his own,' said Caleb. 'What can we do for you, Mr Wilberforce?'

'We?' queried the minister. 'Have you assumed some sort of position of authority in this town? Perhaps the council have made a decision in my absence.'

'The council's decided nothin',' muttered Luke. 'But then they never do, you ought to know that, bein' a member yourself.'

'Then just who has given this man the authority he apparently assumes?' demanded Wilberforce.

'He ain't got no authority,' replied the sheriff. 'You probably heard that he is a bounty hunter as well as a preacher an' both you an' I know that bounty hunters are a law unto themselves.'

'Yes, I heard that,' said Wilberforce. 'In my book bounty hunters have to kill from time to time. How do you explain the obvious juxtaposition, *Mr Black,* if you know the meaning of the word?'

'Being placed side by side,' replied Caleb with a broad grin. Wilberforce looked rather surprised. 'Just because I'm the colour I am does not mean that I am uneducated, *Mr Wilberforce.* I can explain it quite easily. You must know yourself that earning a living by being purely a minister of the church is not easy and most have to supplement their income in some way. Since I do not have a regular ministry of my own, my need is even greater. Several years ago I discovered that I had the knack and the talent to seek out and apprehend outlaws, so I simply turned my ability to my advantage. I do not find that it clashes with my religious calling in any way. Does not the Bible teach us an eye for an eye? How do you supplement your income, Mr Wilberforce?'

Wilberforce looked very uncomfortable and was silent for a moment. 'Certainly not by taking up the gun, *Mr Black*,' he said eventually. 'I am also the town undertaker, which is, in my view, more compatible with my calling.'

'Each to his own, Mr Wilberforce,' said Caleb. 'I dispatch them, you bury them. Whatever my reasons for doing what I do, I believe that everyone in town agrees that somebody has to do something about Black Bill.'

'We employ a sheriff for just that purpose,' said Wilberforce. Caleb simply shrugged. 'That brings me to the reason for being here,' he continued. 'I understand that you have apprehended two of Black Bill's men?'

The sheriff nodded. 'Whilst I agree that something needs to be done about Black Bill and his men, I hope you realize the implication of your action.'

'Reverend,' sighed the sheriff, 'you sound just like the rest of 'em. I've known you shout loud enough about it at council meetin's but when somethin' is done, you run scared. Just what the hell do you want me to do?'

'I expect you to make certain that this town is protected,' said Wilberforce. 'Very well, Sheriff, you are the law in this county and I must accept that you know what you are doing. However, you can rest assured that if anyone is killed, you must accept full responsibility.'

'Maybe you'd better have this badge right now,' said Luke, unpinning his sheriff's star and offering it to the minister.

'If it were left to me I would accept it,' said Wilberforce. 'Perhaps if you were a more regular attender at church I might think differently. However, it is not up to me. You have started something and it is your duty to see it through.'

'And the best way I can do that is if people like you leave me alone,' snapped Luke. 'Yes, I have started something and I do intend to see it through, with the help of the Reverend Black.'

'Very well,' snorted Wilberforce. 'I shall, of course, bring up the matter at the next council meeting and you can rest assured that I shall be calling for your dismissal.'

'You have that right,' said Luke. 'I might even resign before then.'

Wilberforce sneered and looked at Caleb. 'As for you, *Mr Black,* I consider you a disgrace to the ministry, if you are indeed an ordained minister. In my opinion you are no more than a disciple of the devil.'

'An opinion I have heard before,' said Caleb. 'I am past worrying about such accusations.'

'Very well,' snarled Wilberforce, 'do your devil's work. I shall pray for you. I doubt it will do any good though.'

'They do say that the devil looks after his own, Mr Wilberforce,' replied Caleb, with a broad smile. The Reverend Wilberforce snarled and slammed his way out of the office. 'I do believe he does not approve of me,' said Caleb when he had gone.

By the time it was midday and the stage had arrived there was still no sign of Black Bill. As was normal, the arrival of the stage attracted some considerable attention, most people looking for mail or parcels. It seemed that as time had elapsed, a good portion of the townsfolk had almost convinced themselves that Black Bill was not going to show up. Apparently emboldened by this thought, they had emerged from their homes. There were no passengers destined for Beresford and only one leaving, Horst Schultz, the gun salesman.

Beresford was also a staging post for the stage and, as horses were being changed, the relative peace was suddenly interrupted by the arrival of a young man from one of the outlying farms. He was plainly very agitated and immediately sought out the sheriff.

'Black Bill!' he gasped as he crashed into the office. 'He's on his way, I just seen him.'

'How far?' asked Luke, grabbing his rifle.

'When I saw him, maybe five miles,' panted the young man. 'Him, Sioux an' Jake Smith. I got here as fast as I could. I don't think they saw me an' they didn't seem in that much of a hurry.'

'I suspect that they are riding slowly so that someone will see them and tell us,' said Caleb. 'I have seen such tactics many times. Announce your arrival well in advance in the knowledge that panic will spread. It usually works in small towns like this.'

'An' it looks like it's workin' this time,' muttered Luke.

Already many anxious townsfolk had gathered on the boardwalk outside the office and two of them burst into the office demanding to know just how far away Black Bill was. The sheriff did his best to pacify them but nobody seemed to be listening. The two men went outside and announced that the outlaw was on the edge of town. Immediately almost everyone was running and shouting.

Even the change-over of the horses for the stage suddenly stopped as the two men with the horses also fled. The five passengers and the driver were left stranded. Caleb and Luke ventured out into the street, leaving Ted to guard the prisoners. He had been instructed that he should release the prisoners rather than risk his life.

'I reckon you folk had better make yourselves scarce,' Luke told the passengers and the coach-driver. 'It looks like there's goin' to be a delay.'

'This is all your fault!' yelled the gun salesman, Horst Schultz, at Caleb. 'I have a very important meeting in Laurenstown tomorrow. If you hadn't interfered this would never have happened. Miss Greaves was right, folk like you are not to be trusted.'

'Maybe we saved your life, Mr Schultz,' said Luke. 'Our information is that they were plannin' to rob the stage.'

'You can't possibly know that,' snarled Schultz. 'If I am not at that meeting in Laurenstown and lose sales as a result, I shall hold you personally responsible.'

'You do that, Mr Schultz,' said Caleb. 'You can send your bill to my head office.'

'And where is that?' demanded Schultz.

'Just send to the Good Lord,' said Caleb, laughing. 'Now do as the sheriff says and make yourself scarce, there's liable to be some trouble and we don't want anyone getting hurt.'

Horst Schultz quickly muttered some very unChristianlike and certainly derogatory comments about Caleb's colour but was quick to join the other passengers as they crowded into the hotel which was used as refreshment rooms for the stage company. Several anxious faces appeared at a window.

'What now?' asked Caleb as he glanced around the now deserted street.

'I was kind of hopin' you'd tell me,' said Luke. 'I reckon you're more experienced in things like this than me.'

'We don't know if he knows about me or not,' said Caleb. 'For the moment I think we must assume that he does not. I know it's laying you open, Sheriff, but I suggest that you take up position outside your office and wait for him. Whatever you do don't draw your gun, that will only give him an excuse to shoot you. I shall be across the street, behind that water butt.' He indicated a large water butt at the end of an alley. 'Don't worry, if I think he's going to shoot I'll make certain that he doesn't. Just remember, don't give him any excuse to shoot you.'

'I hope for my sake you know what you're doin', Reverend,' said Luke, with a weak grin. 'I don't know about puttin' my trust in the Lord. Like the Reverend Wilberforce said, I ain't never been much of a church-goer, but I guess it's a case of puttin' my trust in His servant.'

'Personally I'd put more trust in my ability to shoot straight,' replied Caleb. 'I haven't yet known a prayer stop a bullet.'

'I feel safer already,' said Luke, once again grinning very weakly. Caleb was uncertain as to whether or not the sheriff was joking.

The street was now deserted and Caleb positioned himself behind the water butt whilst Luke took up his post in a chair outside his office, looking very nervous. From where Caleb was, he had a clear view to the edge of town and slightly beyond. It seemed an eternity before anything happened.

Black Bill and his two remaining men appeared but stopped before they reached any of the buildings. They remained just outside town for a considerable length of time, doing nothing except looking. Eventually all three dismounted and slowly led their horses to a hitching rail outside the livery. Then, at a sign from their leader, the half-breed, Sioux, crossed the street. Black Bill himself took up position in the middle of the street and Jake Smith remained on the livery side. Again they remained motionless for some considerable time before Black Bill waved them forward. Sioux and Jake Smith mounted the boardwalks and all three made their way very slowly towards the sheriff's office.

It would have been a simple matter for Caleb to kill Black Bill there and then and he was very tempted to do so but, strangely, the thought of killing a man in cold blood held him back. Eventually all three were within shouting distance of the sheriff, who was now plainly visible to them.

'You have two of my men,' called Black Bill. 'That was not a very friendly thing to do, Sheriff. Why did you arrest my men?'

'They're wanted outlaws,' called Luke. 'It's my job to arrest outlaws.'

'It is also your job to make sure that no harm comes to any of the citizens of Beresford,' called Black Bill. 'Now you have a choice, Sheriff. You can release my men now and I promise you that no harm will come to you or anyone else. If you don't, I am afraid we shall have to release them by force. If that happens I cannot promise that nothing will happen to you, or anyone else. The choice is yours, Sheriff. Is it worth risking your own life for something you are powerless to stop?'

'They stay where they are,' called the sheriff. 'You can do your damndest.'

'Three against one, possibly two,' said Black Bill. 'I think the odds are in my favour. It appears that the people of Beresford have more sense than you; I don't see anyone to help you.'

'You'll be the first,' said the sheriff. 'I'll make sure of that.'

'Very well, Sheriff,' called Black Bill, raising his rifle and knowing full well that he was out of range of the sheriff's handgun.

There was a single shot and the rifle suddenly spun out of Black Bill's hands as he cried out in pain. Caleb cursed, he had been aiming to kill the outlaw but had missed. He had hit him, there was no doubting that, but plainly not very seriously. He fired again but by that time Black Bill was running towards the boardwalk alongside the hotel and the shot obviously missed its target.

'He's behind that water butt,' called Jake Smith. A volley of shots slammed into the butt and water started to pour out.

'I should have known there *would* be somebody fool enough to take your side,' called Black Bill. 'Sioux, you an' Jake take the bastard out. I want him dead.'

'Cover me!' called Sioux as he crouched low and ran along the boardwalk. Another shot, this time fired by Jake Smith, slammed into the woodwork just above Caleb's head, forcing him to take cover behind the butt.

By that time Sioux had taken cover in a narrow alley almost opposite Caleb and the sheriff had managed to get inside his office. Three more shots ensured that Caleb was pinned down.

'We'll deal with the sheriff later,' called Black Bill. 'Get whoever is behind that water butt first.'

Caleb managed to peer round the water butt and, to his horror, he saw the door of the hotel open and a small, female figure suddenly appeared. It was Miss Greaves, waving nothing more than a rolled up parasol.

'Be off with you, boy!' she shouted at Black Bill, poking him in the ribs. Black Bill was too surprised to stop her. 'You wouldn't dare do anything like this if you were all still slaves.'

'Stupid bitch!' snarled Black Bill, recovering his composure and dragging Miss Greaves in front of him as cover. 'OK, whoever you are behind that water butt, give up now or I kill this stupid woman. You too, Sheriff. Hand over my men or she dies.'

'You wouldn't dare,' called Luke Solomons through the partly open door of his office. 'That'd be murder an' so far you ain't wanted for murder.'

'That doesn't mean I haven't killed nobody,' called Black Bill. 'Are you goin' to take the chance I won't? You, behind the butt, come on out with your hands raised an' you, Sheriff, set my men free.'

'Release them!' The order came from the Reverend Wilberforce, who suddenly marched into the middle of the street. 'I am ordering you to release those men, Sheriff.'

'You keep out of this, Reverend,' called Luke. 'You're likely to get yourself shot.'

'If that is the Lord's will, then so be it,' replied Wilberforce, defiantly. 'The life of Miss Greaves is far more important than keeping those men. In return, Mr Williams,' he said to Black Bill, 'you must release Miss Greaves.'

'She goes free as soon as my men are freed,' said Black Bill. 'And after whoever is behind that water butt gives himself up.'

'He is a fellow of yours,' called Wilberforce. 'Show yourself, Mr Black.'

There was no question of Caleb even attempting to shoot Black Bill and he realized that he was now in an impossible situation. If he remained where he was, it was simply a matter of time before they killed him or, at the worst, Black Bill carried out his threat to kill Miss Greaves. Very slowly he emerged from behind the water butt, his hands raised, his rifle in one hand and one of his Colts in the other. The other Colt remained on his hip. He had to hope that Black Bill would think that the one Colt was all he had and might be able to use the other later.

'Hell!' exclaimed Black Bill. 'A black brother. I ain't never killed a black brother before.'

'I am not your brother,' called Caleb. 'The Reverend Caleb Black, at your service.'

'Reverend!' exclaimed Black Bill. 'Since when did reverends go round shootin' folk? Is this some sort of meetin' of reverends?'

'We just wanted to make sure you had a good send-off,' called Caleb.

'He claims to be a minister of the church,' called Wilberforce. 'I have my doubts about that though. He also claims to be a bounty hunter.'

'Bounty hunter!' snarled Black Bill. 'I hate bounty hunters an' I hate black bounty hunters even worse.'

Black Bill suddenly fired at Caleb. The bullet went wide and Caleb found himself dropping back behind the water butt. Sioux and Jake Smith also fired at the water butt. Caleb saw Jake Smith run along the boardwalk and he somehow managed to get a clear draw on him. He had one chance which he took and Jake Smith cried out in pain as he fell off the boardwalk to the ground, where he remained, apparently lifeless.

Two panes of glass suddenly shattered in

the sheriff's office and two rifle barrels appeared.

'Let her go!' ordered the sheriff. 'Let her go an' you can go free as well.'

'And my men?' called Black Bill, backing along the boardwalk, dragging a struggling Miss Greaves as protection.

'They stay where they are,' replied the sheriff.

'No deal!' called Black Bill. 'They go free as well or she dies.' By that time he was out of sight in a narrow alley.

'He means it,' shouted the Reverend Wilberforce. 'For pity's sake, free those men, Sheriff.'

Caleb noticed that the half-breed, Sioux, had disappeared and he cautiously emerged from behind the water butt.

'What do you think, Mr Black?' called the sheriff.

'I think that perhaps Mr Wilberforce is right,' said Caleb. 'I hate to admit defeat but in this case I do not think we can afford to take the chance.'

'OK,' called the sheriff. 'You hear that, Williams? I'm settin' them free now. We don't have their horses or their guns, they're where they left 'em, down by the river. Now you let Miss Greaves go.'

'As soon as my men are well clear,' called Black Bill.

'They're comin' out now,' shouted the sheriff.

The two men appeared at the door and they both laughed at Caleb as they marched down the street towards their leader. Sioux suddenly appeared outside the livery and led the horses down to meet them. They both mounted Jake Smith's horse. Black Bill emerged from the alley and, dragging Miss Greaves with him, mounted his horse and suddenly pulled her up behind him.

'Let her go!' yelled the Reverend Wilberforce.

Black Bill simply laughed and rode his horse out of town, closely followed by the other two horses.

Caleb ran to the body of Jake Smith and felt for a pulse. 'He's still alive,' he called. 'Somebody get the doctor, quick.'

'What the hell for?' hissed Luke Solomons as he too ran across the street. 'Nobody ain't goin' to lose no sleep if he dies.'

'Do you know where their hideout is?' asked Caleb. The sheriff shook his head. 'Then we need him, we need him to tell us exactly where it is.'

FIVE

The doc declared that the injury to Jake Smith was not as bad as it first appeared, although he had lost a lot of blood. For Jake's own safety, since people were already baying for vengeance, he was kept in jail where the sheriff's wife took care of him. An immediate meeting of the town council was called at which, as he had threatened, the Reverend Wilberforce demanded the replacement of Sheriff Luke Solomons. However, the proposition was soundly defeated, even though the sheriff did offer his resignation. As ever, the purely practical question as to exactly who would replace him appeared beyond any solution. Apart from his deputy, Ted, there did not seem to be any likely candidates. The question of Ted taking over was swiftly settled when he refused.

'So you live for another day,' said Caleb when the sheriff returned and told him. 'At this moment though, there are far more important questions requiring answers. What do they intend doing with Miss

Greaves and what do you intend doing about it?'

'Maybe they've let her go and she's walking back to town right now,' said the sheriff, although he did not sound too convinced. 'I can't see why they should want to keep her.'

'She is apparently a rich woman,' said Caleb. 'The word "ransom" springs to mind. Have you any idea how much money she does have?'

'None at all,' admitted Luke. 'I suppose it is a possibility though. If Black Bill does decide to hold her to ransom, we can expect a message stating how much he wants. In the meantime, what do we do, just sit around and wait?'

'Without knowing exactly where she is, we don't appear to have much option,' said Caleb. 'Jake Smith is still in no condition to talk and I am not too certain that he will say anything when he does recover. These Blue Mountains, do you think it would be possible to find out where their hideout is without Smith telling us?'

Luke shook his head. 'Almost impossible I'd say,' he said. 'You could hide a whole regiment of soldiers up there an' never find 'em.'

'Then it appears that we must wait for Black Bill to make the first move,' said Caleb. 'Let's just hope that it happens sooner rather than later. At least if he does try for a ransom it will give us somewhere to start looking.'

'Black Bill ain't stupid,' said Luke. 'He'll be expectin' somethin' like that.'

'I would be surprised if he did not expect it,' said Caleb. 'However, if he does demand a ransom, he will have to make the first move. I know he will be prepared for just such an eventuality and I would hate to disappoint him.'

'Just remember that it could be a matter of life or death for Miss Greaves,' reminded Luke.

'I realize that,' said Caleb. 'In the meantime I suggest that you form a posse and go through the motions of looking for her. It probably won't do any good, but at least it will make the people of this town think that something is being done and it might send the same message to Black Bill.'

The sheriff laughed drily. 'You're right about it not doin' any good,' he said. 'There is another problem though. As much as they might all shout, I don't think I could raise a posse. Miss Greaves is not a particularly popular figure in Beresford, she's upset most folk in one way or another with her sharp tongue.'

'I know,' said Caleb, laughing. 'I have been on the receiving end of it, remember. I think that you ought to try forming a posse. You already have one volunteer – me.'

'That makes a grand total of two of us,' said Luke, once again laughing drily. 'I can't count Ted, somebody has to stay here just in case somethin' happens while the posse is away. Always supposin' I do manage to find any volunteers. OK, I guess you're right, I have to be seen to be doin' somethin'. I'll go and find out just how many civic-minded folk there really are in Beresford. I don't expect too many.'

The sheriff's prediction of not being able to raise a posse proved accurate. He returned half an hour later with the news that any posse would consist of himself, Caleb and, surprisingly, Sam Boulton.

'I'd hardly call three of us a posse,' he said, with a resigned sigh. 'The only reason Sam Boulton volunteered was because he was shamed into it by his wife.'

'I'm surprised more of the women didn't shame their husbands into it,' said Caleb.

'Oh, sure,' said Luke. 'They were all for it,

providin' their men were not part of it. As one of 'em said, Miss Greaves don't have no man to rely on to provide for her an' no family to worry about either. They all said the same, they didn't want to end up widows just 'cos some old spinster went an' did somethin' stupid. They said it was her own fault for doin' what she did. Personally I'm surprised so many folk saw what happened.'

'So they'd rather see her murdered than try to help?' said Caleb. 'I can't say that I'm too surprised. It might be said that I too have little reason to bother what happens to her after the way she treated me. That, however, is not the way my mind works.'

'Pardon me for bein' cynical, Reverend,' said Luke with a knowing smile. 'But I'd say your prime consideration was sixteen hundred dollars.'

'Eight hundred,' corrected Caleb. 'I have promised you half, remember. That's not quite true, Sheriff. I do care what happens to others. I suppose that in a way you and I are to blame for what happened to her.'

'How so?' asked Luke, looking puzzled.

'If we hadn't arrested those two men this would never have happened,' said Caleb. 'I am probably more at fault than you are, I talked you into doing it.'

'Yeh, if this, if that or if the other,' said Luke. 'It happened an' there's not a damned thing we can do to change it now. The point is that three of us don't really stand a lot of chance out there against them and I sure wouldn't like to rely on Sam Boulton to stay with us if the goin' got rough.'

At that moment Maud Solomons, the sheriff's wife, came through from the cells and announced that Jake Smith had come round. 'Don't be too harsh on him,' she warned. 'He is still very weak and he doesn't seem to really know what's happening.'

'Then he might not realize what answers he's giving us,' said Caleb. 'Come on, let's see what we can get out of him. You had better stand by just in case,' he said to Maud Solomons.

Jake Smith might have come round but, as the sheriff's wife had said, he certainly did not appear to know where he was or what was happening. His response to the questions put by the sheriff and Caleb was to stare at Caleb and announce that he, Caleb, was not Black Bill. After ten minutes he closed his eyes and seemed to slip back into unconsciousness. Just as his eyes closed, he said one word. It was difficult to make out exactly what that word was, but Caleb was convinced it was 'eagle'.

'Eagle!' he said to Luke as they returned to the office. 'Does that mean anything to you?'

'Not much,' said the sheriff. 'It is eagle country up in the Blue Mountains and there is a mountain called the Eagle's Nest but that's about all. I shouldn't think it's the mountain though. I've been up there a couple of times and it rises almost sheer. Only things what can climb that mountain are mountain goats. Nobody in their right minds goes anywhere near it, especially in the winter when it gets snowed up.'

'Which might make the base of it an ideal place for a hideout,' said Caleb. 'Well, you've got one willing volunteer and one not so willing. Do we put on a show of looking for her?'

'It'd be a waste of time,' said Luke. 'The best we can do is for you an' me to ride out an' see if they have released her. We'll go up as far as Parker's Ridge which is about two miles beyond the bridge. If we haven't found her by then I'd say we won't find her.'

'OK,' agreed Caleb. 'It's better than doing nothing. I don't suppose Hooper's and Green's horses will still be where we left them?'

'I shouldn't think so,' replied Luke. 'We can check if you want.'

They met Sam Boulton outside the office and he seemed quite relieved when they told him that his services were not required for the moment.

The ride out to Parker's Ridge did not result in finding Miss Greaves and the subsequent search along the river showed that the outlaws' horses had also gone. Two hours later they returned to Beresford to the news that Jake Smith had apparently taken a turn for the worse and that the doc now had serious doubts as to whether he would survive and was with him at that moment but was not to be disturbed as he was performing an operation.

'There's nothin' else I can do for him,' said the doc when he eventually emerged. 'I wasn't going to take the bullet out just yet since it was not really causing any problem but I decided that I had better do it now. I don't think that either the bullet or my operation is the cause. All I can put it down to is the amount of blood he lost. I did find a vein that had been cut and blood was draining into his body but I've stitched that up. It's up to him now.'

'Thanks, Doc,' said Luke. 'Maud will keep

an eye on him, she knows what she's doin'. Look in later, but if he gets any worse we'll call you.'

It was almost three o'clock when the shout suddenly went up along the street that one of Black Bill's men was heading for town, apparently alone. Even though he was alone, it was still sufficient to cause some considerable panic and the streets were very quickly deserted. Caleb and the sheriff took up position on the boardwalk outside the office and waited. About ten minutes later Saul Green rode slowly into town, obviously aware that his presence had caused panic. He appeared to be enjoying the situation. Caleb and the sheriff stood up to face Green and for a few moments it looked as though the outlaw was prepared to draw his gun. However, he eventually smiled and raised his hand away from his gun.

'You've got some nerve,' said the sheriff as Green moved forward and stopped a few yards from the office. 'Give me one reason why I shouldn't arrest you?'

'The fact that you have to ask such a damn fool question for one,' sneered Green. 'For another the fact that we have that stupid woman, Miss Greaves I think her name is.

I've only known her a short time an' I can see why she ain't never married. No man in his right mind would ever want a woman like that. Spinster or not, you wouldn't dare do anything to me unless you don't mind seein' her dead.' He laughed drily. 'Personally I wouldn't blame you if you did.'

'OK, so what do you want?' demanded the sheriff.

'Black Bill reckons her doin' what she did was probably the best thing that happened,' said Green. 'He reckons she's a wealthy woman an' worth a lot of money alive. You can have her back in return for five thousand dollars. Personally I wouldn't give even five dollars for her.'

'Five thousand!' exclaimed Luke. 'Where do you expect us to find that kind of money? I doubt if this town could raise even five hundred.'

'Five thousand,' Green sneered again. 'Not one cent less. Black Bill reckons she's got at least that much on her own. How you raise the money ain't no concern of ours. Five thousand is the price. Maybe you should get the money from the bank, it is her money.'

'We can't expect the bank to hand over five thousand of her money just like that,' said Caleb. 'Bankers are peculiar people, they like to have everything above board. They like to have lots of pieces of paper with signatures which, in this case, means that he will have to have authorization from her.'

'Then it looks like you have a problem, Mr Bounty Hunter,' said Green. 'Mind, if I was in your shoes I'd say good riddance to her. She's been nothin' but a pain in the ass ever since we took her. Only woman I ever met what don't seem to give a shit about Black Bill or even her own safety. She insists on callin' him "boy" an' it's beginnin' to get through to him. He says nobody has called him that since he ran away from a plantation somewhere's down South. He didn't like it then an' he sure don't like anyone callin' him that now. He says that white kids young enough to be a man's grandson used to call all black men "boy". Imagine that, callin' your own grandpa somethin' like that.'

'I can appreciate how he feels,' said Caleb. 'OK, supposing we do get the money, what do we do with it?'

'You take it out to Parker's Ridge, on your own, Sheriff,' replied Green. 'If there is any sign at all that you are not alone, the deal is off and she dies.'

'When?' asked Luke.

'Black Bill is a reasonable man,' said Green. 'He'll even put up with her an' her mouth until he gets the money. He knows you can't just whistle that kind of money out of thin air so he's prepared to give you until noon the day after tomorrow. Just remember that if you don't show up – alone – she dies.'

'So far,' said the sheriff, 'none of you is wanted for murder. You just remember that if anything happens to her you'll be hunted down. I'll have to bring in a US marshal and they usually win. I think the marshal for this part of the state is Brett McCormack an' he's got one hell of a reputation.'

'For a share of five thousand I for one will take that chance,' said Green. 'With Jake out of the way there's a bigger share for the rest of us. By the way, what happened to Jake, is he dead?'

'No, he's alive and well,' said Luke. 'He took a bullet but he's OK and ready to talk. When he does there will be no place in this state where you can hide.'

'With more'n a thousand dollars in my pocket I won't hang about too long,' said Green. 'I guess that goes for the others as well.'

'And Mrs Greaves?' asked Caleb. 'I assume

she will be handed over when the sheriff delivers the money?'

'Somethin' like that,' said Green. 'At least you'll be told where you can find her. Don't you worry none, Black Bill is a man of his word if nothin' else. If he says she's safe then she's safe.'

'No deal,' said Luke. 'If I do manage to get the money I must insist that she is handed over at the same time.'

'Sheriff,' said Green, laughing, 'I don't think you quite understand. We hold all the aces, you ain't in no position to demand nothin'. I've told you the terms. I've nothin' more to say 'ceptin' if I don't get back, she dies anyhow, so don't even think about arrestin' me.' He turned his horse and glanced back over his shoulder. 'Give my regards to Jake, tell him it was nice knowin' him.'

'So he's expendable,' said Caleb. 'Black Bill got you out of jail, don't you think he owes it to Jake to do the same for him?'

Saul Green laughed. 'Five thousand split four ways is a whole lot more'n five thousand split five ways. As far as I'm concerned Jake can take his chance with the law. He ain't wanted for nothin' too serious so a short turn in prison won't hurt him. Anyhow, he's too young, he needs to learn a few things an' he was becomin' somethin' of a nuisance to all of us.'

'I'll tell him that,' said Luke. 'I don't think he will like it.'

'I don't give a shit what he likes or doesn't like,' called Green as he spurred his horse forward. 'You have until noon the day after tomorrow, Sheriff.'

Saul Green had hardly reached the end of the street before people started to reappear. Amongst them was the Reverend Wilberforce, who marched straight across to Luke and Caleb demanding to know exactly what was said. Tom Gittins and two more members of the town council also arrived. Luke called them into his office but the Reverend Wilberforce insisted that Caleb should not be allowed to hear what was being discussed. Caleb chose not to push the matter and withdrew.

'And does Miss Greaves have that kind of money?' asked Wilberforce.

'Nobody except her and the bank knows how much she has,' said Luke.

'Then we had better find out,' said Wilberforce. 'I suggest we go along to the bank and find out and arrange for the money to be withdrawn.'

'If you say so, Reverend,' said Luke with a resigned sigh. 'Tell me somethin' though. If it was anyone else, someone who didn't have two cents to rub together, such as old Mrs Dobbs, what would you do?'

'The question does not arise, Mr Solomons,' said Wilberforce. 'If it was somebody such as Mrs Dobbs I doubt very much if he would be demanding five thousand dollars in ransom.'

'Why not?' asked Luke. 'Mrs Dobbs is still a human being and a man like Black Bill wouldn't worry about where the money came from. Just supposin' it was somebody like Mrs Dobbs and he demanded five thousand dollars, would you allow her to die or try to raise the money?'

'But it is not Mrs Dobbs,' said Wilberforce, stiffly. 'It is Miss Greaves. Come along, we are wasting time. Mr Sylvester is still at the bank.' They marched down the street to the bank where they found the president of the bank, James Sylvester, singularly uncooperative.

'This is most irregular, gentlemen,' intoned Sylvester. 'Most irregular and quite impossible. The law is quite specific. I cannot divulge the state of any of my customers' accounts without their consent and

I certainly cannot withdraw funds without written consent.'

'This is an emergency, Mr Sylvester,' said the sheriff. 'Her life depends on that ransom being paid.'

'Then I am afraid that you will have to find some other method of obtaining the money,' insisted Sylvester. 'The only exception to the rule would be if I was ordered to do so by a circuit judge and in my experience judges are very reticent to make such orders. In fact I have never known any judge make such an order other than where someone has died without leaving a will and I can assure you that Miss Greaves has left a very specific will.'

'And the circuit judge is not due here for another three months,' said Luke.

'Look at it this way,' said the Reverend Wilberforce. 'It is her money and I am quite certain that under the circumstances she would be only too ready to sign the necessary documents. It is her life, after all.'

'You could be right,' agreed Sylvester, 'but we don't know that for certain. Miss Greaves is a very independent woman, you must know. She is not the most popular of women in Beresford, of which she is well aware, which is why she does not expect anyone to do anything for her. By the same token she rarely helps others. I am sorry, gentlemen, but in the absence of her authority or the order of a court, there is nothing I can do.'

'But she does have the money?' asked Wilberforce.

'You are a minister of the church, Mr Wilberforce,' said Sylvester. 'From time to time people must confide in you. Do you not regard such confidences as sacred?'

'Of course,' replied Wilberforce, 'but that is different.'

'Is it, Mr Wilberforce?' asked Sylvester. 'I submit that any knowledge I may gain from my position is just as sacred.'

'But we need to know that she could repay the money should we be able to raise it,' insisted Wilberforce. 'You surely can't expect the town to pay?'

'Why not, Mr Wilberforce?' replied Sylvester. 'Surely it is one function of the town council to protect its citizens in the best way it can. Once again, I am sorry but there is no way I can help.'

'And that is your final word, Mr Sylvester?' asked Wilberforce.

'My final word,' said Sylvester. 'Now, gentlemen, I do have work to attend to. As you well know, Mr Gittins, your work does not stop when the doors of your establishment have closed and the last customer has departed. In fact I venture to say that that is the time when the real work begins. It is the same with a bank. There are payments and withdrawals to be entered and books to be balanced.'

'So what do we do now?' asked Tom Gittins when they stood on the boardwalk outside the bank. 'We can't just leave her to be killed by Black Bill no matter what our opinion of her might be. I don't think even her worst critics would expect us not to do anything.'

'Perhaps he will not kill her,' said Wilberforce. 'I believe that it is all bluff on his part. I think you will discover that he will release her when he finds that there is no ransom forthcoming.'

'Are you really prepared to take that chance, Reverend?' asked Luke.

'Unless you can find five thousand dollars, it seems to me that we have little choice in the matter,' said Wilberforce. 'Perhaps you can raise the money, Mr Gittins? Establishments such as yours are responsible for the debts many folks incur. Perhaps now is the time to repay them.'

'I am certainly not responsible for anyone's debts,' growled Gittins. 'I don't force anyone to drink my beer or take their pleasures with my girls. Another thing, Miss Greaves has certainly not contributed towards my business. In fact if it was left to her, she, like you, would have me closed down.'

'Yes, she does have her good points,' said Wilberforce with a wry smile. 'Ah well, in a perfect world... However, perhaps it is as well that the world is not perfect. If it was, I would be out of business. Well, gentlemen, we have done our best and I suggest that any further action is now a matter for our esteemed sheriff and his new-found friend, the so-called Reverend Caleb Black.'

'At least he's ready to do somethin',' muttered Luke. 'Which is more than can be said for the likes of you and certain other people I can think of. Caleb Black is a minister, I know he is, I've seen proof, but at least he admits that prayer has never yet stopped a bullet. OK, I guess it is up to me to do somethin'. Just you remember what you said, Reverend, don't stand in my way, that's all.'

The sheriff returned to his office and told Caleb what had happened. Caleb admitted that he had not expected anything to come of the meeting and that he had spent his time studying a map of the area including the Blue Mountains.

'How long would it take me to get up there?' he asked.

'The Eagle's Nest?' said Luke. 'Five or six hours, maybe even longer, I ain't too sure. Best man to tell you that is Eli Goodman, he's a fur trapper an' knows those mountains like the back of his hand.'

'Why didn't you tell me about him before?' asked Caleb.

'I never even thought about him,' admitted Luke. 'I don't even know if he's in town. If he is, I'll guarantee he's blind drunk somewhere. He lives in a tumbledown hovel out by the rubbish dump. How the hell he manages to put up with the stink an' the flies I'll never know, but then he don't smell too wholesome himself so maybe even the flies find him a bit too much.'

'Then the best thing I can do is see if he's at home,' said Caleb.

'There's one sure way of getting' him to talk,' said Luke. 'Just wave a bottle of whisky in front of him.'

'I think I can afford a bottle of cheap whisky,' said Caleb. 'Perhaps if I made that a decent bottle of Scotch it might loosen his tongue even further. Who knows, perhaps he might even take me up there.'

'For two bottles he'd lead you to the ends of the earth,' said Luke, with a broad smile.

SIX

Having purchased two bottles of Scotch whisky, Caleb headed for the town rubbish tip which was well away from most buildings, although there were one or two sorry-looking shacks actually on the tip – which appeared to be lived in. Caleb had been told that Eli Goodman's hovel was the one almost in the centre of the tip. As he had been warned, the smell and the flies were almost overpowering and he did think twice about going to see Eli. Apart from the flies, there were countless rats feeding on the waste along with numerous birds of all sizes. The presence of rats and birds did not surprise Caleb, but he was not prepared for the greeting outside Eli Goodman's shack.

Seemingly out of nowhere, a large brown bear suddenly reared in front of him, its huge arms outstretched as if about to attack. Instinctively his Colt was in his hand, although he realized that his bullets were most unlikely to stop the animal unless his shot was extremely accurate. As he took careful aim, the bear roared and dropped on all fours, turned and ambled away. He breathed a sigh of relief but waited until the animal was well away.

There did not seem much point in knocking on the rickety door as it gave way when he touched it. Once inside he found the smell even worse than that outside and he gasped for breath. He could just make out the shape of a body on what he supposed was a bed. He wondered if the smell was the result of the body having decomposed. However, a grunt and a movement confirmed that it was still alive.

'Whaddyawant?' grunted the untidy bundle. 'Can't a man get no peace round here?' The figure slowly raised itself on to one elbow, stared at Caleb for a moment and then grabbed at a bottle on the floor. After taking a long drink, he wiped his hand across his face and sat up. 'Ain't you that black feller what's come into town? Yeh,' he continued, answering his own question. 'I seen you this mornin'. You're supposed to be a preacher ain't you? What can I do for you, Reveren'? If it's my soul you is after, forget it, old Lucifer had first claim on me years ago.'

'I take it you are Mr Eli Goodman?' said Caleb. 'No, I am not after your soul, I am after your help. By the way, did you realize that there is a large bear right outside your door?'

'Arthur!' said Eli, laughing coarsely. 'Yeh, Arthur. Sure, I suppose you could say he belongs to me. Leastways I brought him up since he was a cub. You don't have to worry about him, he ain't never hurt nobody yet.' He got off the bed, scratched himself and spat on the floor and then took another drink from his bottle. 'Did you say you wanted my help?' He laughed coarsely. 'Now there's somethin', a preacher wantin' help from old Eli. Yeh, that sure is some-thin'.' He took another drink and wiped his dirty sleeve across his mouth. 'Now I reckon help is somethin' that has a price, Reveren'. The more help you want, the greater the price. Somethin' to do with what some educated English feller once told me was the law of supply and demand. You demand an' I supply, at a price.'

'Is there anywhere else we can talk?' asked

Caleb, gagging at the smell. 'Even outside would be better than in here.'

'In here's fine by me,' grunted Eli, picking up what was apparently a fur coat and putting it on. 'Arthur's ma,' he grinned, stroking the matted fur. 'I don't normally kill bears with cubs but she had got herself caught in one of my traps an' her leg was almost off so I thought it best to finish her.' He picked up the bottle, took another drink, held it up to what light there was and cursed. 'Last bottle too,' he grumbled. 'You don't happen to have the price of a bottle of whisky on you?'

'Better than that,' said Caleb, taking one of the bottles from his pocket and holding it up for Eli to see. 'Best Scotch.'

'You sure know how to get round a feller, Reveren',' said Eli, casting the empty bottle to one side. It shattered as it hit a pile of other discarded bottles. He made a grab for the whisky in Caleb's hand.

'Not so fast,' said Caleb, pulling the bottle out of his reach. 'First I want to know if you can help me. Mind you, looking at you and this place, I have serious doubts.'

'You drive a hard bargain,' muttered Eli. 'OK, so what do you want to know? I don't see how I can help you though. Nobody ever asks old Eli for anythin', especially help.'

'I am told that you are a trapper,' said Caleb. Eli nodded and pointed at a pile of skins and furs. Caleb realized that that was where the foul smell originated. 'I am also told that you work the Blue Mountains.'

'Ever since I was little more'n a boy,' slurped Eli, hardly able to keep his eyes off the bottle in Caleb's hand. 'Ain't nobody knows them mountains better'n I do.'

'That is what I had hoped,' said Caleb. 'You must know the mountain they call the Eagle's Nest.'

'Eagle's Nest! Sure I know it. I ain't never been up it though. No man in his right senses wants to climb that thing.'

'I don't want to climb it,' said Caleb. 'I just want you to guide me there. Just the base of it will do.'

'Take you there?' said Eli. 'Reveren', so far you've used up half that bottle in your hand, takin' you out there will take a whole lot more.'

Caleb smiled and handed Eli the bottle. Eli immediately opened it and took a long drink. He sighed with obvious pleasure and sank back on the bed.

'Now that's what I call whisky,' he sighed, holding the bottle up. 'Maybe you can

111

explain why the Scotch folk never did learn to spell. Whiskey should be written with an e but for some reason Scotch whisky don't have the e. Why is that?'

'That, I am almost ashamed to admit, is one of life's mysteries for which there is no obvious answer,' admitted Caleb. 'I am surprised that you can read.'

'Read!' snarled Eli, obviously annoyed at the suggestion. ''Course I can read. I was educated by some monks an' they made sure we all could read an' write. They used to beat the hell out of us if we got it wrong. OK, Reveren', so you want me to take you up to the Eagle's Nest. Maybe I will, maybe I won't. It all depends.'

'Depends on what?' asked Caleb.

'On what's in it for me for a start,' said Eli. 'For another, exactly why you want to go up there. That's bad country. Oh, the bears and wolves ain't no bother, I can deal with them anytime, it's that Black Bill what's the trouble.' He looked at Caleb and laughed. 'Do you know about him, Black Bill? He's a negro, just like you, except that he ain't a preacher. He's got a camp up there, him an' his men.' He laughed again. 'One of 'em is called Sioux, a half-breed. Yes, sir, a half-breed who never knew who his father was.'

112

He laughed coarsely and tapped the side of his nose. 'Old Eli knows who his pa was though.'

'I wouldn't be surprised if you do,' said Caleb. 'You have just earned yourself another bottle of Scotch.' He took the other bottle from his pocket and threw it on the bed. 'There's plenty more if you will take me up there.'

'When?' said Eli, grinning as he picked up the second bottle and caressed it.

'Now,' said Caleb.

'Now!' exclaimed Eli. 'At this time of day? No, sir. I can't just get up an' go like that. I need time to prepare.'

'I can't think what preparations you need to make,' said Caleb.

'Mr Preacherman,' said Eli, 'right now I'm too damned pissed to go anywhere an' thanks to you that's how I'll be for the rest of the day.'

'How long will it take to reach Black Bill's camp?' asked Caleb.

'Now we have the truth of it, Mr Preacherman,' said Eli with a broad grin. 'You want me to take you to Black Bill. Now this wouldn't just happen to have somethin' to do with that old spinster woman, Miss Greaves, would it? I hear tell that Black Bill has kidnapped her.'

'And I intend to rescue her,' said Caleb. 'With or without your help. How long will it take?'

'Now that all depends on whether you take the easy route or the hard route,' said Eli. 'The easy way takes maybe a day, the hard way about half a day if you're lucky an' dependin' on what time of year it is an' you ain't scared of heights.'

'How long will it take going the hard way tomorrow?' asked Caleb.

'Providin' the weather holds out, half a day, like I said,' muttered Eli. 'I hope you know what you're doin', Reveren'. Black Bill ain't a feller to be tangled with at the best of times.'

'That is my problem,' said Caleb. 'You will take me up there?'

Eli shrugged. 'Now like I said, that all depends on what's in it for me an' providin' you don't expect me to do any fightin'. Bears an' wolves I can tackle but Black Bill is a different matter.'

'I won't expect you to do anything other than take me up there,' said Caleb. 'As for payment, I suggest half a dozen bottles of Scotch would be just about your price. Payments to be made when we get back.'

'If you get back alive,' muttered Eli. 'I'd like payment up front, just in case.'

'Very well,' agreed Caleb. 'I shall arrange for six bottles at the saloon. I do not want you drunk when we go.'

'You don't have to worry none about me,' grunted Eli. 'When I'm not out huntin' or trappin' I get drunk, I admit it. When I'm out there though, there's not a drop passes my lips. You got yourself a deal, Reveren'. I'll be stone cold sober when we leave in the mornin'.'

'Then we are agreed,' said Caleb. 'We start out at dawn.'

Caleb went outside and took a deep breath. Even the stench of the rubbish was like a breath of fresh air compared to that inside the cabin. He returned to town wondering if he was doing the right thing or not.

The man Caleb met the following morning was a totally different man from the one he had met the previous day, at least in manner. The dirty clothing, the matted hair and beard might have been the same, but it was plain that Eli Goodman was true to his word and was sober. Eli had already saddled his mule and, without saying a word, he mounted up and waved Caleb to follow. Once again, Caleb had serious doubts as to whether or not they would reach the Eagle's Nest in the half day promised. In his experience mules were notoriously slow.

An hour after leaving Beresford and still not having spoken, Eli indicated a small river crossing the main trail and turned to follow it upstream. It seemed to lead directly to a sheer cliff, but Caleb had to assume that Eli knew where he was going.

'Now we start the hard climb,' said Eli, speaking for the first time. 'This is the hardest part, after that it's a bit easier.'

At first they climbed very steeply, still following the course of the river which was now little more than a fast-flowing stream, skirting various waterfalls and rapids. Eventually the river suddenly disappeared and they were faced with what seemed to be an unclimbable rock-face towering at least 300 feet. Eli saw the look on Caleb's face and laughed. He turned between two large rocks, pointed upwards and indicated that they should dismount.

There was a very narrow fissure which seemed hardly wide enough to allow a man to pass through, let alone a mule and horse. Eli laughed once again and led his mule into the gap. For about twenty or thirty yards it was indeed a very tight squeeze for both man and animal, but suddenly it widened. Caleb looked up and sighed as he faced what seemed to be an almost sheer climb.

'A month ago we wouldn't've been able to come this way,' said Eli. 'This would've been full of water and impossible.'

'If you don't mind me saying so,' said Caleb, 'it looks impossible now.'

'Just keep climbin',' said Eli with a coarse laugh.

They continued to climb and Caleb was quite surprised. By taking a zigzag course it proved a lot easier than it appeared. Even so, it was very slow going and, according to Caleb's watch, it had already taken over an hour since they entered the fissure and there still appeared to be at least as far to go again. However, he was proved wrong as the fissure suddenly gave way to a narrow, flatter but very deep gully. They followed this gully for about another half-hour before Eli led them up the side and on to more open, if still very rocky and hilly, country.

'That's the worst bit done with,' said Eli. 'There's still some climbin' to do but apart from makin' sure you don't fall, it's a lot easier. The next bit is a narrow ledge just about wide enough to take a horse.' He laughed coarsely again. 'I hope you an' that horse of yours have a head for heights. It's about two hundred feet straight up an' about three hundred feet straight down an' it ain't too often that a man falls uphill. I maybe should've told you to change your horse for a mule. Horses is more intelligent than mules an' they sense danger more an' panic a bit more. Mules is different, I don't think they've got a brain in their head. It don't matter to them if a track is six inches wide or six feet.'

'I can appreciate just how a horse feels,' said Caleb.

Twenty minutes later they reached the narrow ledge Eli had been talking about and once again Eli dismounted and led his mule. Caleb also dismounted. Although Caleb had anticipated the worst, it was not quite as narrow as he had expected. For the most part it was at least three feet wide, but as they progressed, it narrowed to about eighteen inches in a few places.

Caleb had never been unduly worried about heights, but after a time a certain fascination took over. He had heard that faced with such conditions, some men developed an urge to throw themselves off the edge and he had to admit that he too, for some strange reason, was beginning to develop that urge. His horse seemed to be suffering from the same condition and he had to keep it on a tight rein. The mule and Eli, on the other hand, simply plodded on, heads down.

Even allowing for their slow progress, the journey along the ledge seemed never-ending and, according to Caleb's watch, it took them just under one hour to reach the end of it. Caleb had to admit to a great feeling of relief as he stepped out on to more solid, open ground.

For a brief time they moved downhill, but Caleb had the feeling that this respite was purely temporary and he was proved correct when once again they had to negotiate a narrow trail which rose steeply up the side of a mountain. The trail might have been narrow, but it was not quite as narrow as the ledge and the drop was not a sheer one, although it was still very steep. At the top of the track Eli stopped and pointed ahead.

'The Eagle's Nest,' he announced, indicating a high peak. 'Highest mountain in the Blue Mountains. We're about half way now. I reckon we made good progress an' made up some time. I don't normally travel that fast, ain't no need.'

'And hopefully past the worst,' said Caleb. 'Are you sure we'll make it in half a day from Beresford? It looks a long way to me.'

'Yes, sir, I'm sure,' said Eli. 'It's easy goin' from here on. Hardest part is droppin' down into the valley up to Black Bill's camp.'

'I thought there might be another hard part,' sighed Caleb.

'There's a small lake about a mile up ahead,' said Eli. 'We'll stop there an' rest for a while.'

'I'd rather carry on,' said Caleb.

'Maybe you'd rather keep goin', Reveren',' said Eli, 'but your horse an' my mule need a rest an' some water. We stop for a while.'

Caleb could tell from the tone of the trapper's voice that it was no use arguing with him and when they did stop alongside the lake, he was almost glad of the rest himself. The water was very clear, very cold but tasted wonderful. He had expected Eli to produce a bottle of whisky but he seemed content with water. He looked at Caleb and smiled.

'I knows what you're thinkin', Reveren',' he said. 'No, I ain't brought no whisky. You've seen what it's like out here. A man wouldn't survive an hour if he fell an' I long since learned that whisky is the worst thing for makin' any man lose his balance. I gotta admit that I don't normally work high up like we are now. There ain't no bears, no wolves, no beaver, in fact not much at all 'ceptin' mountain goats an' they're not much use for anythin'. All the rest is further down. Only thing I come up here for is stoats. Stoats change the colour of their fur in winter from brown to white. Trouble is it's the white fur what folk really want. Ermine I think they call it. I hear it's in great demand for them fancy men an' women back East. They're worth huntin' though; two white furs can keep me in whisky for a week or more.'

'If you don't mind me saying so,' said Caleb, 'it seems a rather pointless existence. All this trouble collecting furs just to spend on whisky.'

'Life is pointless,' said Eli. 'A man sweats an' toils all his life an' for what? A better place to live, money in the bank which most is too scared to spend, raisin' kids what don't give a shit about you. What good do you think you really do with all your preachin' an' talk about heaven, Reveren'? No, sir, life ain't got no point at all, but we're here for some reason an' I suppose we have to make the best of it in whatever way we think best.'

'Very profound,' said Caleb. 'Perhaps you should tell that to Miss Greaves. I doubt she would agree with you.'

'Maybe not,' agreed Eli. 'OK, Reveren', let's get goin' or she might not get the chance to agree or disagree.'

For more than another hour the going was quite easy and even Eli's mule seemed to travel faster than mules normally did. Eventually they were overlooking a valley, the floor of which was some two or three hundred feet below them. Eli pointed up the valley.

'Black Bill's camp used to be up there,' he said. 'Probably still is. He's picked a good spot. He can see anyone comin' up the valley long before they reach him. Only trouble is it gets snowed up in winter.'

'And we have to go down there?' asked Caleb. 'Is there no way we can approach his camp without being seen?'

'Like I said,' said Eli, with a broad grin. 'There ain't nobody knows these mountains better'n I do. There ain't no way from up here but I knows a way round. Don't you worry none, we won't be seen.'

The climb down into the valley was slow and tortuous and more than once Caleb felt in danger of falling. However, they eventually made it to the valley floor where, instead of going up the valley, Eli led Caleb across and started to climb the opposite side.

'This way brings us up behind their camp,' explained Eli. 'It'll take about another hour.'

'At least they will not be expecting us from behind,' said Caleb. 'You don't happen to know the layout of their camp do you?'

'Layout?' said Eli with a laugh. 'Nothin' much to it. They're in a cave. It looks down the valley. Now there's someone who lives a pointless life,' he continued. 'He robs folk, rapes women, sometimes he robs the stage an' for what? He sure as hell can't spend his money up here. At least I don't have to keep watchin' my back just in case someone like you is out to kill me.'

'Who said anything about killing?' asked Caleb.

'So what else are you goin' to do with him?' asked Eli. 'I can't see him just agreein' to let you take him back to Beresford so's you can throw him in prison. For all I know you might be one hell of a good preacher but I don't think even you could persuade

Bill to give himself up.'

'I can be very persuasive,' said Caleb.

'Yes, Reveren',' said Eli with a coarse laugh. 'I seen your guns. I'll bet you can be very persuasive holdin' them to a man's head. That's one thing what has been puzzlin' me. You're the first preacher I ever seen what carries guns. Somehow that tells me that preachin' ain't all you do.'

'You seem to know most things,' said Caleb. 'I'm surprised that you didn't know that I am also a bounty hunter.'

If Eli was surprised, he certainly did not show it, simply nodding and smiling. 'Maybe I should've guessed,' he said. 'It does explain why you is so damned keen to get your hands on Black Bill. I reckon Miss Greaves ain't that important to you.'

'That, my friend, is where you are quite wrong,' said Caleb. 'If it was just the reward for Black Bill and his men I wouldn't bother. There's only sixteen hundred dollars out on them all and I would not put myself to all this trouble just for that.'

'Sixteen hundred!' said Eli, whistling softly. 'If I could get my hands on that much I'd never need to trap another animal. I could keep myself in whisky for the rest of my life.'

'And it would be a very short life,' said Caleb. 'How old are you?'

Eli laughed and gazed up at the sky. 'Well now, that's somethin' I don't really know, Reveren'. Even my ma didn't know what year I was born, but then she didn't know much about anythin', poor cow. I tried workin' it out once an' the nearest I could get to it was about sixty-five, an' that was a couple of years ago. A short life, Reveren'? I reckon I already outlived most folk in these parts. Only one what's older is old Widder Jefferson an' they reckon she's over ninety. She must be too. When I was a boy I remember her bein' in her thirties with two kids. Both of them have been dead a long time now.'

'Then isn't it about time you retired?' asked Caleb.

'Retire!' exclaimed Eli. 'What the hell for? I ain't got no money to keep me. Besides, I seen folk what have retired an' they all died within a couple of years on account of they had nothin' to live for. Huntin' an' trappin' is my life. One day I'll go off into the mountains an' never come back an' that's fine by me. At least the buzzards won't go hungry for a couple of days.'

Caleb let the matter drop and they

continued in silence for a while. Eventually Eli turned off the ridge along which they had been travelling and pointed back down the valley.

'Black Bill's cave is back there,' he said. 'About half a mile. You can't miss it. I hope they've got Miss Greaves there otherwise you've come all this way for nothin'.'

'I hope so too,' agreed Caleb. 'It could be that they've already taken her down to Parker's Ridge. That's where the exchange was due to take place tomorrow at noon.'

'Exchange?' queried Eli. 'What are you talkin' about?'

'I thought you might have known,' said Caleb. 'They have offered to free her for five thousand dollars.'

'Five thou...' whistled Eli. 'Hell, I suppose a man has to think big sometimes. Where you goin' to get that kind of money?'

'We can't,' admitted Caleb. 'That's partly why I am up here now.'

'I get it,' said Eli. 'No money, no Miss Greaves. I reckon he would kill her too. I wish you the best of luck Reveren'. From now on you is on your own. I'll stay here an' wait for you. I'll be able to see an' hear if anythin' happens.'

'I don't think I need tell you not to get

involved,' said Caleb. 'Just in case I don't make it, it's been a pleasure knowing you.'

'Somehow I get this feelin' that you is goin' to make it,' said Eli. 'I'll be waitin' for you.'

SEVEN

Caleb left his horse with Eli and clambered down the steep slope. He did not worry too much about being seen or heard since the cave was apparently about half a mile away and because they would not be expecting anyone – if they were indeed expecting anyone – to come in from above them. The valley floor was well strewn with large rocks which gave plenty of cover if he should meet with any opposition.

When he thought he was close to the cave, Caleb became rather more cautious and chose to circle wide of where he thought the cave was. Eventually he caught sight of four horses, which confirmed that all the outlaws were still there. It also confirmed that Miss Greaves must still be there. He settled behind a large boulder about fifty yards away, from where he could see what was going on, and waited.

At first there was no sign of anything other than their horses, but after about ten minutes two figures emerged from the cave. The one was plainly the half-breed, Sioux, and the other proved to be Saul Green. They appeared to be collecting wood and for a moment he thought that they were going to head towards him, but they turned away.

He took sight of the pair along his rifle but did not shoot. It was more than possible that he could have taken out either man, but he doubted if he could take out both and even if he could, there were still two others in the cave. He lowered his rifle knowing that any precipitate action by him might easily result in Miss Greaves being killed. Although he was sure that she was in the cave, he wanted to make certain before doing anything.

Getting closer to the cave was out of the question from where he was. The only chance he had was to approach from the opposite side and even from that side he would have difficulty. He looked at his pocket-watch which told him that it was 3.30, about another three and a half hours until sunset.

The presence of Miss Greaves was confirmed when she appeared briefly at the entrance to the cave. She gave the impression of being well in control of herself, standing erect, pointing at something and snapping at Sioux. The half-breed even seemed to be slightly afraid of her and apparently did as she had instructed. Caleb smiled. He could well imagine that Miss Greaves had all but assumed command. Having satisfied himself that she was safe and well and that he was not, at that moment, in a position to help her, Caleb decided to return to Eli.

'I think the best chance I have is to try to get to her after sunset,' he said to Eli. 'She seems to have plenty of freedom to come and go almost as she pleases.'

'I reckon you know what you is doin',' said Eli. 'Only trouble with goin' in after sunset is that you won't be able to see much. Sure, they won't be able to see you either, but then neither will she. Once the sun's gone down it gets pretty damned dark down there an' the moon won't be high enough to help for a couple of hours at least.'

'Then what do you suggest?' asked Caleb.

Eli shrugged. 'Nothin', I'm used to huntin' animals, not people,' he said. 'It seems to me most of the animals seem to know I ain't out after them this time as well.' He pointed across the narrow valley. 'Wolves,' he said. 'They know we're here but I reckon they know we ain't out to kill 'em.'

'I don't see any,' said Caleb, shielding his eyes.

'They're there,' assured Eli. 'Keep watchin' an' you might see 'em among the rocks. I reckon they're attracted by the horses.'

'Our horses?' asked Caleb.

'I shouldn't think so,' said Eli. 'More likely the horses down by the cave.'

'I see them,' said Caleb. 'Three of them at least.'

'More like nine or ten,' said Eli. 'Yeh, thought it was. See that big, grey old male standin' on his own?' Caleb nodded. 'I call him Whitefoot on account of he's got one white paw at the front. They don't normally come this high up. I reckon they've come up lookin' for mountain goats but caught a scent of the horses. The deer they usually feed on have already moved further down in readiness for winter settin' in so the wolves is lookin' for other food. They don't move when the deer do on account of each pack has its own territory an' normally they never go on another pack's territory. They only do that when the snow drives 'em down.'

'I only hope they don't come up here looking for an easy meal,' said Caleb.

'They won't,' said Eli. 'They know we're here though but I ain't never known any wolf attack a man. I heard stories, but I reckon that's all they are, put about by folk what don't know no better.'

'I'll take your word for it,' said Caleb. 'I was going to cross the valley and down to the cave. I'd rather not chance it for the moment.'

Eli smiled but looked thoughtful. 'Now seein' them has given me an idea,' he said. 'If we get behind 'em, we can drive 'em down the valley an' with a bit of luck they'll run straight for the cave.'

'And what purpose will that serve?' asked Caleb.

'It'll cause a distraction,' said Eli. 'I don't know what them outlaws know about wolves but I reckon it's probably about the same as most folk – not a lot. Tell me somethin', Reveren'. If you was down there an' you suddenly found yourself in the middle of a wolf pack, what would you do?'

'Either shoot my way out or try to scare them off,' said Caleb.

'But you wouldn't just stand by an' wait for 'em to move on?' Caleb shook his head. 'An' I reckon them down there will do the same. I know they've been up here for some time but I don't think they will have had much in the way of dealin's with wolves or bears. The wolves know they're there too an' will keep clear. Like I say, this pack is usually about five miles further down. They've only moved up recently.'

'And you think that if we drive them down to the cave it might give me a chance to get Miss Greaves out of there?' said Caleb. 'I wish I had your confidence.'

'Confidence ain't got nothin' to do with it,' said Eli. 'I just reckon it's about the best chance. Have you got any better ideas?'

'None at all,' admitted Caleb. 'My only thought is if something goes wrong it means they will know we are here.'

'They've got to find out sooner or later,' said Eli. 'I reckon it'd be better sooner, that's all.'

'Very well,' said Caleb, with a deep sigh. 'So how do we go about driving those wolves down?'

'We go further up an' work our way down,' said Eli. 'Now just remember what I said. Wolves won't attack people so don't you go lettin' off at 'em, no matter what they do. Sure, they'll growl at you an' bare their teeth, but that's all they'll do. Providin' you don't give ground they'll soon turn an' run.'

'I bow to your superior knowledge,' said Caleb. 'I only hope this works. If it doesn't there's no knowing what they'll do to her or if we'll get another chance.'

'Just trust me,' said Eli. 'OK, we go up as far as that big outcrop…' He pointed at a large rock jutting out of the side of the valley. 'All the wolves is below us right now. When we get there, you take the far side, drive any wolves you see ahead of you an' then work your way round to the cave. I'll try to make sure the wolves keep movin' towards the horses.' Caleb was not at all certain that Eli's plan would work, but in the absence of any better ideas, he had to agree.

Ten minutes later, both men were in position but about fifty yards apart. At a signal from Eli they started moving forward. Despite Eli's assurance that the wolves would not attack, Caleb had his rifle at the ready. He had heard before that wolves would not attack a man, but he had never really been sure if he believed it or not and had never before been in a position to put it to the test.

For the first sixty or seventy yards there was no sign of the animals, but Caleb suddenly caught sight of one of them as it ran between two rocks. He glanced at Eli who seemed to be signalling that others were also ahead of him. With his heart in his mouth and his rifle gripped tightly, Caleb moved forward.

Reaching the two rocks where he had seen the wolf, Caleb very cautiously moved between them and breathed a deep sigh of relief when he did not encounter the animal. However, his relief was short-lived when he suddenly heard a growl.

A large wolf was looking at him, about twenty feet away and Caleb had to quell his instinct to shoot the animal. For a few seconds they stared at each other, Caleb breaking out in a cold sweat and the wolf baring its teeth. Suddenly the animal turned and fled and Caleb almost sank to the ground with relief. He forced himself to continue moving forward. By that time he had lost sight of Eli and the one line of comfort.

He realized that he must have moved ahead of Eli as suddenly he found himself almost surrounded by snarling wolves.

Despite Eli's assurances, at that moment Caleb feared for his life. He raised his rifle and took aim at the largest and seemingly most aggressive wolf.

'Just keep movin' forward!' Eli suddenly hissed beside him. 'We've got 'em on the run.'

'They certainly don't look as though they're running as far as I'm concerned,' whispered Caleb. 'Are you quite sure they won't attack?'

'As sure as I can be,' replied Eli. Caleb was not reassured. Eli raised his arms and growled at the animals and, much to Caleb's relief and surprise, they turned and ran. 'OK, I can deal with 'em from here on,' said Eli. 'You make your way round to the cave. I'll give you ten minutes before I drive 'em down.'

Caleb was quite relieved to get away from the wolves and made his way along the side of the valley as fast as he could, using the many large rocks as cover. Eventually he found himself overlooking the cave and about twenty yards from it. Three of the men, Black Bill, Sioux and Saul Green, were sitting outside the cave. There was no sign of Hooper or Miss Greaves.

Suddenly the horses, which were about

ten yards further away, started to neigh and snort, each pulling at their tethers. The reason for their sudden panic appeared in the form of three of the wolves. Black Bill saw them at the same time as he did.

'Wolves!' Black Bill called. 'They're after the horses. Hoppy, get on out here.' Hoppy Hooper appeared at the mouth of the cave, closely followed by Miss Greaves. Black Bill fired a shot in the direction of the wolves and all four were racing forward towards their horses, their guns firing. The wolves turned and fled but the four men continued to run after them. Caleb did not stop to think. He also ran towards Miss Greaves and grabbed her.

'Come on,' he commanded. 'While we've got the chance.'

'*Mr Black!*' she cried. 'Unhand me. What *do* you think you are doing?'

'There's no time to explain,' hissed Caleb. 'Just do as I say.'

'I most certainly will not!' she said, struggling to free herself from his grasp. 'Unhand me, I say, unhand me.'

Caleb glanced in the direction the outlaws had gone and there was no sign of them. 'Miss Greaves,' he hissed. 'Don't you want to be saved? Now do as I say, come with me.' He dragged her after him and was very surprised at the resistance she offered. However, she eventually seemed to realize that she was fighting a losing battle and her struggles died down. He managed to get her amongst the rocks and glanced back just in time to see the outlaws returning, congratulating themselves on a job well done.

At first the men did not seem to realize that their hostage was missing. It was not until Hoppy Hooper went into the cave, calling to tell Miss Greaves that the danger was averted, that he realized she was gone.

'She ain't here!' called Hooper, running out.

'She has to be,' said Black Bill. 'Even she wouldn't be stupid enough to go out when there's wolves about. Are you sure?'

'Sure I'm sure,' rasped Hooper. 'She ain't here I tell you.'

'She must've run scared,' said Saul Green. He looked up at the rocks behind the cave, seemingly directly at Caleb, who, at that moment, had his hand clamped firmly over Miss Greaves's mouth. 'It's OK,' called Green. 'You can come back now, there ain't nothin' to be scared of.'

'I think she is trying to escape,' said Sioux. 'Well she won't get far,' said Black Bill with a coarse laugh. 'You might as well come back here now,' he called. 'There ain't nowhere you can run or hide.'

In the meantime Sioux was studying the ground and, looking very serious, turned to Black Bill. 'She is not alone,' he said. 'There has been somebody else here. See,' he continued, pointing at the ground. 'She has struggled. She has small feet and there are marks made by much bigger feet.'

'Don't be stupid,' snarled Black Bill. 'Who the hell could've got up here? We didn't see nobody.'

'The signs are clear,' insisted Sioux. 'It also explains why those wolves suddenly appeared. I think they were a distraction. Wolves do not normally go anywhere near men if they can avoid it. I think they were driven here to lure us away.'

'That bastard of a bounty hunter!' snarled Black Bill. 'It has to be him, there ain't nobody else got the nerve to come out here.' He stared up at the rocks for a few moments and then called out. 'OK, Black, or whatever your name is. I know you're up there. I've got to admit that it was a nice idea to drive those wolves down. I congratulate you an' it just goes to prove that us black folk ain't so stupid. What would be stupid is you thinkin'

138

you can get her out of here. There ain't nowhere for you to go. Now you just be a good preacherman, send her back an' we'll leave you to get the hell out of here.' There was silence from Caleb. 'I'm goin' to give you one last chance, Reveren',' Black Bill called again. 'If she don't come back in the next five minutes we're comin' after you an' pretty soon you'll be a dead preacherman.'

Caleb allowed his grip on Miss Greaves to relax slightly and whispered to her, 'I'm going to take my hand off your mouth,' he said. 'Don't do anything silly like calling out. I am not here for my health, I am here to take you back to Beresford. I am well aware of your opinion of me and all black men and that it must be abhorrent to you for my black skin to be touching yours. Despite whatever I might think of you and your beliefs, I *am* here to rescue you. Now you won't do anything stupid will you?' She stared at him with obvious hatred for a moment and then shook her head. 'Good,' said Caleb. 'I might be a minister of the church, Miss Greaves, but I am also a man and I have the same instincts for survival as any other man and if that means your life or mine, then I am afraid you will be the loser.' He slowly took his hand from her mouth.

'Am I a sop to your conscience?' she said. 'If it hadn't been for you I would not have been here in the first place.'

'My conscience has nothing to do with it,' said Caleb. 'The only reason you are here now is because you think all negroes are second class. If you had stayed in the hotel instead of poking Black Bill with your umbrella, you would not be in this position. Now, I take it that you do not want to return to Black Bill?' She shook her head. 'Then you must do exactly as I tell you. Any moment now they are going to start looking for us and when they do there is liable to be shooting. You just keep your head down and let me deal with them. Do you understand?'

'I understand that you think all women incapable of using a gun,' she said. 'That is not something exclusive to black men, most white men think exactly the same.' She suddenly snatched one of Caleb's Colts from its holster and, before he could say or do anything, had expertly cocked it and aimed it at his head. For a brief moment Caleb thought that she was going to shoot him, but she allowed herself a fleeting smile and lowered the gun. 'It might interest you to know, Mr Black, that I am an extremely good shot with both pistol and rifle. If we are going to put up a fight then two guns are better than one. Besides, you wouldn't like to leave a defenceless woman to the mercy of men like those, would you?'

'I am quite certain that you would never be defenceless,' he said. 'That tongue of yours is quite capable of whipping anyone into line. Very well, keep the gun, for the moment, but just make certain that every shot counts.'

'As strange as it might seem, Mr Black,' she said, 'this is not the first time I have been faced with such a situation and I am still alive to tell the tale.'

'I can well believe it, Miss Greaves,' said Caleb. 'Now, follow me, I have a friend waiting further up.'

Caleb was quite surprised at the speed and agility with which Miss Greaves moved as they dashed from rock to rock. He looked back to see the four outlaws also darting between rocks. After about a hundred yards they were faced with a large expanse of open ground and he knew that the outlaws were closing in fast.

'We'll never make it across there,' he said. 'The time has come to make a fight of it. Are you ready?'

'As ready as I'll ever be,' said Miss Greaves.

'As my old father used to say, wait until you see the whites of their eyes.'

'Something like that,' conceded Caleb.

It was Caleb who fired first, sighting a sudden movement about twenty yards away. He knew that his shot has missed, but it did have the effect of making the man dive for cover. Miss Greaves fired too and Caleb had to admit that she did handle the gun like an expert. There were two shots in response, one of which ricocheted off a rock close to Miss Greaves's head but she appeared completely unmoved.

'That was close,' she said with a laugh. 'You know, I haven't had as much fun as this in ages.'

'I'd hardly describe being shot at as fun,' said Caleb. 'Don't you realize that they are trying to kill you?'

'Oh, they won't kill me,' she replied in a matter-of-fact tone. 'I'm far too valuable to them alive. It's you they're trying to kill.'

'And as far as I'm concerned my life is far too valuable,' said Caleb. He looked across the open space. 'Somehow we have to get over to those rocks,' he said. 'If we can do that it will mean that we can pin them down on this side.'

Miss Greaves looked and nodded. 'Then,

142

Mr Black, I suggest that we make a run for it.'

'The only problem with that is, as you say, they will try to kill me, not you,' said Caleb. 'I'm not scared of dying, but I'd rather not die just yet.'

'Then we sit here and wait for them to pick us off,' she said. 'I thought you said you had a friend. Where is he?'

'I wish I knew,' muttered Caleb. Another shot ricocheted off a rock close to Caleb and it was plain to him that the outlaws were closing in. He made a sudden decision. 'OK, we run for it,' he said. 'When I give the word, you run just as fast as your old legs and that skirt of yours will allow.'

Miss Greaves laughed and suddenly hitched up her skirts and tucked them into her bloomers. 'Not very elegant,' she said, 'but I can run a lot faster if they aren't in the way. I'm sorry if I've shocked you, but I expect you've seen a lady's underwear before. Well, what are we waiting for?'

'Nothing,' said Caleb. 'Let's go.'

Suddenly they were both running across the open ground, which was about 100 yards wide. Their flight was given impetus by a volley of shots, most of which fell well short but one or two bullets did raise dust around them. Caleb was very surprised that she was able to keep up with him. Several more shots hastened them on their way but they made it and both flung themselves behind a large boulder. Immediately they were both firing, forcing the outlaws to retreat to the safety of the rocks on the opposite side. Whilst Caleb's bullets carried the distance, those fired by Miss Greaves fell well short.

'Reload!' ordered Caleb, pulling six bullets from his gunbelt and handing them to her. 'You'll never hit them from this distance, so leave any shooting to me and my rifle.' He reloaded his Winchester. 'So far, so good,' he continued. 'I have to hand it to you. You might look like a frail old woman but it just goes to prove that looks can be very deceptive.'

'I've had to look after myself most of my life,' she said. 'There have been others who thought I was too old, too frail and, more annoying, a woman. Six of them never lived to tell the tale. Yes, Mr Black I have killed men before. The thing is we can't stay here. Where is this friend of yours?'

'I told him not to get involved,' said Caleb. 'He's an old man. Mind you, it was his idea to drive those wolves down to the cave.'

'So you're stuck with one old man and an old woman,' she said, laughing. 'Not very good odds against four men in their prime.'

'I've had better odds,' admitted Caleb. Quite unexpectedly there were several shots from somewhere to their right obviously aimed at the outlaws. Caleb laughed. 'It looks as though the cavalry has just arrived.'

'Cavalry, Mr Black?'

'Well, it looks like Eli has disobeyed orders and got himself involved,' he said. Caleb looked across at the outlaws and was very surprised to see them retreating. 'Well done, Eli,' he said. 'They're on the run. Come on, the horses are over on the other side. We shouldn't have any trouble reaching them.'

'You don't think that's the last we've seen of them do you,' she said, more as a statement than a question. 'It is a long way back to Beresford.'

'But at least we'll have a horse and a mule to ride on,' said Caleb.

'A mule!' she exclaimed. 'Just who is this friend of yours?'

'Eli Goodman,' said Caleb. 'Hunter and fur trapper. He knows these mountains better than any man. If anyone can get us back to Beresford, he can.'

'Eli Goodman!' said Miss Greaves. 'I can't

say that I really appreciate your choice of friend, Mr Black. I have never seen him sober and he smells terribly.'

'Right now Eli is stone cold sober,' assured Caleb. 'As for his smell, there's nothing I can do about that. I'd rather put up with his admittedly unsavoury body odours and habits than a bullet from one of them. I hope you remember to thank him for his timely intrusion.'

'I shall do no such thing, Mr Black,' she snorted, pulling her skirts out of her bloomers. 'I am very particular as to the company I keep.'

'At this moment in time I'd say you don't have much choice in the matter,' said Caleb. 'You're stuck with a negro, and a smelly drunkard. We all have to make sacrifices, Miss Greaves, and mine is being forced to save someone with the extreme views and beliefs which you possess.'

'*Touché*, Mr Black,' she said. 'Well, since I have to endure such company, I suppose I had better make the best of it.'

There was no sign of Black Bill and his men as Caleb and Miss Greaves made their way across the valley. Eli was waiting for them.

'Told you it'd work,' he said with a certain smug satisfaction. 'The pity is they're still

out there. Good afternoon, Miss Greaves,'
he said, raising his battered hat to her.
'Sorry I couldn't get to you sooner.'

'You did your best, I suppose,' she conceded, sniffing the air. 'I would appreciate it
if you remained downwind, Mr Goodman.'

EIGHT

'We shall have to make our way back the
easy way,' said Caleb. 'We can't expect Miss
Greaves to negotiate the way we came, it's
far too difficult.'

'Please don't make any concessions to me
simply because of my age,' objected Miss
Greaves, 'and certainly not because I am a
woman. I can assure you that I can cope
with anything a man might be faced with. I
was brought up to fend for myself and you
have seen for yourself that I am quite
capable of handling a gun.'

'I have no doubt that you were,' said
Caleb, 'and you are plainly able to use a
gun. Nevertheless, I must insist. If nothing
else I believe it would be safer especially
since we have gone to all this trouble to get

you back. I would hate to lose you in some other way after all this.' He addressed Eli. 'You know the territory, is there any way we can avoid Black Bill?'

'It might take a bit longer but I reckon it's possible,' said Eli. 'Only problem is I don't know how well they know these mountains, 'ceptin' I know Sioux was born an' raised in these parts.'

'Then that's settled,' said Caleb. 'We shall have to take the chance. Now, Miss Greaves, I am afraid that you have to make a choice. You can ride up behind either Eli or me. I am well aware of your feelings towards negroes, so Eli does have the advantage in that he is white.'

'Apart from the fact that mules are just about the most uncomfortable animal I can think of to ride,' she replied. 'I do not think I could stand Mr Goodman's decidedly unsavoury body odours. You are also quite wrong about my feelings towards negroes, Mr Black. I was raised by a black nanny and a nicer woman I have yet to meet. If you can put up with me, I dare say I shall survive the experience of riding with you.'

'Body odours!' grunted Eli, looking at Caleb. 'Is that another way of sayin' that I smell?'

'I would suggest that is putting it mildly,' said Miss Greaves. 'I am sorry to be so blunt, Mr Goodman, but that is the way I am. Perhaps you ought to make the acquaintance of soap and hot water rather more often.'

'No offence taken,' said Eli with a broad grin, 'but I did have a bath about three months ago so I shouldn't smell that bad. Anyhow, like you say, mules ain't the most comfortable of animals to ride 'specially ridin' up behind.' He looked up at the sky. 'We'll never make it back tonight,' he continued. 'There's a place not too far from here where we can hole up.'

'What about Black Bill?' asked Caleb. 'Won't he be expecting something like that?'

'Who knows,' said Eli with a shrug. 'That's a chance we'll have to take.'

'We could ride through the night,' suggested Miss Greaves.

'Ma'am,' said Eli, 'have you any idea just how cold it gets up here, even in the summer?' She shook her head. 'Well I can assure you it sometimes get cold enough to freeze the marrow in your bones. Black Bill knows that too, an' I agree he won't be too keen to go lookin' for us once it gets dark but it's bad enough tryin' to find your way in daylight. When it's dark there's places where you can't tell if somethin' is a shadow, a small hole or a deep gully. We rest up in a cave I know.'

'I suppose that you know best, Mr Goodman,' conceded Miss Greaves. 'Come, Mr Black, help a lady up.'

Caleb mounted his horse and reached down to haul her up behind him and was rather surprised when she put her arms around his waist.

At first Eli led them away from the route back to Beresford but after about twenty minutes he led them through a narrow gully which seemed to head more or less in the right direction. As far as Caleb was concerned the gully presented an ideal opportunity for Black Bill to ambush them and, when he mentioned this fact to Eli, even he had to concede that they would stand little chance should he do so. Despite this he did not seem unduly concerned. Caleb, however, placed his rifle across his legs and kept a constant look-out.

Reaching the end of the gully proved to take far longer than Caleb had expected. This was due in part to the gully being longer than he had expected but in the main to the fact that travelling was rather slow due to the numerous rocks and large boulders. By the time they did reach the end of it, the light was beginning to fade quite quickly. Eli assured them that the cave was only about another half-hour. True to his word, it was exactly half an hour later when he called a halt outside the cave.

'There's a few trees down there,' said Eli, pointing down the narrow valley. Caleb could just make out the tops of some trees. 'There's a water-hole too,' continued Eli. 'You go collect some wood, Reveren'.'

'Wouldn't it be better to stay down by the water-hole?' asked Miss Greaves.

'Sure, if you don't mind bears an' wolves for company,' said Eli. 'Wolves wouldn't be much of a problem but bears is kinda particular an' they object if they find strangers blockin' the way to their water an' there's no knowin' just what they'll do. Sometimes they'll just ignore you but sometimes they'll charge an' when they do you'd better move darned quick. I seen one rip a mule to pieces in no time at all. Normally bears keep to their own territory but for some reason there's allus quite a few of 'em round here. No, ma'am, the cave's the safest place.'

'Don't bears live in caves?' asked Caleb.

'Sure,' said Eli, 'but they like proper caves, this one ain't nothin' more'n a hole in the rock. Don't you worry none about bears, the fire'll keep 'em off. You just make sure there ain't one of 'em down by the water-hole.'

'I'll take my rifle just in case,' said Caleb.

'Might as well take a kid's pea-shooter,' said Eli with a coarse laugh. 'I seem more'n one bear take the full contents of three rifles an' hardly flinch. If you do have to shoot at one, just make sure you hit it right between the eyes.' With these reassuring words ringing in his ears, Caleb went in search of wood.

The night passed without incident from either Black Bill or bears, although both Caleb and Miss Greaves were quite convinced that a bear had spent the night prowling round just outside the cave and the horse had been very restless. The mule had not made a sound. The presence of a bear seemed confirmed when Eli pointed at scuff marks.

'Looks like a big feller too,' he said. 'I reckon it was an old grizzly I've been trackin'. Wily feller what lets you get so close but no closer.'

'Will it still be around?' asked Miss Greaves.

'Shouldn't think so,' said Eli. 'He's sleepin' up somewhere now I reckon. OK, let's get started. Barrin' hold ups an' Black Bill, we should be in Beresford by about six tonight. Sorry there ain't nothin' to eat.'

'I've gone several days without food before now,' said Caleb. 'What about you, Miss Greaves?'

She smiled slightly and patted her stomach. 'It will do me good to starve for a while,' she said. 'I do believe I have been putting on weight lately. I would appreciate a drink of water though.'

'We'll stop down by the water-hole,' said Eli. 'Once we get down a bit, water shouldn't be no problem.'

It was about midday when Eli became obviously uneasy. At first Caleb tried to ignore it, mainly because he did not want to frighten Miss Greaves. However, as they approached some woods which were about 300 yards away, even she noticed Eli's rather strange behaviour.

'Do you have a problem, Mr Goodman?' she asked. 'I have noticed you acting rather strangely for the past few minutes.'

Eli stopped and looked around. 'Do you

153

ever get the feelin' that you're bein' followed or somebody is lookin' at you?' They both nodded. 'Well I've had this feelin' for about the past half-hour. I'm certain that somebody has been doggin' us an' I reckon that it can only be that half-breed son of mine, Sioux.'

'A son of yours, Mr Goodman?' queried Miss Greaves.

'Yeh, ma'am,' replied Eli. 'That no-good half-breed is my son. Just take my word for it, it'll take too long to explain. He's inherited the Indian ways from his mother over mine.'

'And what makes you think it is him?' asked Caleb.

'Oh, nothin' I can put a finger on,' said Eli. 'If it had been one of the others I don't think they would have been able to keep themselves hidden so effectively. Just take my word for it that somebody is doggin' us. I ain't never been wrong yet.'

'And you believe that the others might be waiting for us in those woods?' said Miss Greaves. 'If that is so, Mr Goodman, how did they get there before us?'

'You got it in one,' said Eli. 'I might be wrong but them woods is the ideal place for an ambush. As for gettin' there before us, there's about three ways they could've done. Remember we headed north first, so they had a start on us.'

'So what do we do?' asked Caleb. 'Is there another way?'

'Take your pick,' replied Eli, indicating ridges either side of them which bypassed the woods.

'Either way, if they *are* in those woods, they might see us,' said Caleb. 'If they don't, the one who is following will. What is over those ridges?'

'That one on the right has a sheer drop of about two hundred feet,' said Eli, 'an' the other has a drop of more'n fifty feet sheer.'

'So we would have to ride along the top,' said Caleb. 'We would be sitting targets.'

'That's just about the size of it,' said Eli. 'So it looks like we have a choice of bein' sittin' targets on top of one of the ridges or ride on through the woods not knowin' if they're behind the next tree.'

'And what would be your choice, Mr Goodman?' Miss Greaves asked.

'Me, I'd turn round an' go back,' said Eli. 'Only problem with that is I reckon it's just puttin' off the inevitable. Black Bill ain't about to give up so easy. I suppose I'm for goin' through the woods. I reckon if I can

155

hear an' smell bears an' wolves before I see 'em, I can do the same with people. Even people have their smells.'

'I am fully aware of that fact,' said Miss Greaves, pointedly sniffing the air.

'I'm not so sure,' said Caleb. 'If we're out in the open we can at least see where they are and what we are shooting at. I don't suppose for one moment that they are out to kill you, Miss Greaves, but you could easily be killed or seriously injured in the crossfire or by a ricochet.'

'But they will not hesitate to kill either of you,' she reminded. 'Mr Black, I would point out the obvious and remind you that I am not a young woman. I have had a good, long life and I doubt that I have very many more years ahead of me. I am not afraid of dying, even by a bullet. I also have to tell you that I have not had as much excitement as this in many a year. Let me have one of your guns and some extra bullets and we shall see just how determined these men are.'

'Now that's what I call a *real* woman,' said Eli with genuine admiration.

'Yes, Mr Goodman,' said Miss Greaves with obvious pride. 'A *real* Southern woman.'

'Very well,' conceded Caleb, with a resigned sigh. 'I know when I am beaten.'

He handed her one of his two Colts and pulled another six bullets from his belt which she put in a pocket in her dress.

'Thank you … Reverend,' she said, for the first time acknowledging the fact that he was an ordained minister. 'Perhaps it is time to pray to the Lord.'

'Pray to the Lord indeed,' agreed Caleb. 'However, I think ammunition will definitely be far more useful at this moment. Unfortunately I have yet to be convinced that the power of prayer can deflect a well-aimed bullet.'

'I'll say amen to that,' said Eli. 'I guess I'm kinda like Miss Greaves, I'm livin' on borrowed time too. Let's go.'

'I assume that the wood is only as wide as this valley,' said Caleb. 'How far down the valley does it go?'

'About four miles, I reckon,' said Eli.

'And the track goes right through the middle I suppose,' continued Caleb. 'Is there any point in skirting round the edges?'

'Not much,' said Eli. 'Nothin' but rock, wet moss an' fallen trees an' the trees are so close together an' the moss so thick it's almost impossible to move. Down the middle there's fewer trees an' not so many rocks.'

'Fewer trees mean less places for them to hide,' said Caleb in an attempt to reassure Miss Greaves but at the same time realizing that he was also reassuring himself.

They proceeded towards the trees at a very leisurely pace but all three of them were concentrating hard on detecting any sign of the outlaws. The trees were eventually reached without any incident and when they passed beneath the first one, Eli indicated that they should ride well apart.

'This way one of us might stand a chance,' he said. 'I reckon we're safe enough for the moment, 'specially since they weren't waitin' for us at the start.'

'Is there anywhere in particular they might wait?' asked Miss Greaves.

'I was just thinkin' about that,' said Eli. 'Sure, I reckon if it was me layin' an ambush I'd choose a place about half a mile ahead. The trail passes alongside a river an' alongside a small cliff. Immediately after the cliff it widens out into a basin. It ain't that big but it is the one place where they could get above us.'

'Is there no way round?' asked Caleb.

'Not with a horse or mule,' said Eli.

They were passing several very large fallen trees and Caleb suddenly stopped and pointed at the fallen trees.

'I have an idea,' he said. 'There looks to be enough space to hide the horse and mule among that lot. Miss Greaves could stay here and keep an eye on them and also for whoever is following us. Eli, you and me could go forward on foot to this basin and surprise them. If they are not there we have lost nothing except time. I take it we will be able to get above the basin if we don't have animals to think about.'

'Easy enough,' agreed Eli. 'OK, I'm for it, it sure beats ridin' into an ambush.'

'And don't think we are giving you the easy option, Miss Greaves,' said Caleb before she could object. 'It is vital that someone should protect the only means of transport we have and also to take care of whoever might be following.'

'Thank you, Mr Black,' she replied. 'You are quite right. Besides, I am neither built nor dressed for climbing. Don't worry about me.'

The animals were quickly hidden, and Miss Greaves took up a position from where she could see along the track but not be seen too readily. She took a couple of sightings along the barrel of the Colt and, with an expertise which even Caleb admired, soon acquired a feel for the weight of the gun. Satisfied that she was as safe as she could be, Eli and Caleb started off to find Black Bill.

Almost immediately, Eli led Caleb up the hill and Caleb soon realized just why it would have been impossible to take either the horse or mule. After a very short time the moss-covered rocks, fallen trees and low-hanging branches made it very difficult for even someone on foot. The result was that forward headway was painfully slow and Caleb lost all sense of just how far they had travelled. Eli on the other hand almost seemed to be enjoying himself.

They had been climbing steadily for some time when Eli suddenly crouched and pointed down. Caleb crouched alongside him but try as he might he could neither see nor hear anything.

'I can't even hear any birds,' whispered Caleb.

'Precisely,' whispered Eli in response. 'No birds means somethin' has scared 'em off an' I don't think it was us. The basin is just down there. Now if I'm right Black Bill an' the other two will be on the top of it. The best thing we can do is for one of us to go straight down an' for one of us to circle round to that big tree an' then down.'

'You go straight down,' said Caleb. 'I'll make my way over to that tree. Give me five minutes to get into position.'

'You got it,' whispered Eli. 'Just make sure you don't tread on any dry branches. Somethin' like a twig snappin' can be heard for a hell of a long way.'

'I can float if I have to,' said Caleb with a broad grin.

Caleb very quickly discovered that it would have been better if he had been able to float. There were numerous twigs and branches, a great many hidden under the thick moss, and avoiding them proved very difficult. Those twigs and branches above the moss, although there were a great many of them, proved fairly easy to avoid. The problem was that he soon discovered that there were many more beneath the surface. They had had the same problem earlier, but the necessity for silence had not been so acute. More than once, when treading on apparently nothing but moss, he had heard a distinct cracking as a hidden twig gave way. However, he eventually reached the tree and glanced back. Eli was nowhere to be seen.

On the assumption that Eli had already moved down, Caleb also continued down the now quite steep slope. If anything the moss became even more wet and slippery and Caleb had some difficulty in preventing himself from sliding and falling.

According to Eli, the basin was just below but the dense cover made seeing anything clearly very difficult. It was as he stepped on one of the few bare rocks that he realized that he was standing on the edge of the basin. He quickly withdrew behind a tree, crouched and peered around, hardly daring to breathe. Realizing that his Winchester was not suited to what appeared to be close-quarter fighting, he quietly slipped his remaining Colt from its holster.

At first there was nothing to be seen or heard and he was beginning to wonder if Black Bill was there. His gut instinct however, told him that he was not alone and he did not think it was the presence of Eli. A slight movement a few yards to his right, the opposite direction to that in which Eli would have been, confirmed the presence of at least one man.

Ideally he would have liked to have been able to talk to Eli but that was out of the question. In effect he was on his own and would have to act accordingly. Another slight movement to his left indicated the presence of someone else, which could have been either Eli or one of the outlaws. He had to assume that it was one of the outlaws.

He could just make out the opposite side of the basin but was unable to tell if there was anyone else there. He was just considering his next move when whoever was on his right suddenly stood up. He immediately recognized Saul Green.

Without thinking, Caleb raised his Colt and immediately fired.

In the relative silence of the forest, his shot sounded like a clap of thunder. Saul Green yelled out and collapsed. Caleb knew that he had hit him. Almost immediately there followed a volley of shots, all apparently being fired at imaginary targets, along with someone shouting, 'They're behind us!'

With nothing obvious to aim at, Caleb held his fire. Silence descended briefly as the others also held fire. Suddenly there came the sound of someone crashing through the undergrowth followed by more shouting. Eventually all sound ceased for some time.

'Very clever, Reveren',' came the voice of

Black Bill, apparently from some distance away. 'OK, so you got the better of us for now, but it's a long way back to Beresford.'

'I think there's one less of you now,' called Caleb. 'I know I hit Green.'

'Sorry to disappoint you,' replied Black Bill. 'Sure, he took a bullet but he ain't hurt that bad. Just remember what I said, it's a long way back to Beresford. I don't know how you knew we was here, but your luck can only last so long.'

'Long enough to see you behind bars, I hope,' called Caleb. 'If you don't find me, I'll find you.'

'I don't think so, Reveren', I don't think so.'

Once again silence descended and this time Caleb had the feeling that Black Bill and his men had moved on.

'Eli!' he called. 'Are you OK?'

'Sure am,' called Eli from quite close by. 'Pity you had to shoot when you did, I had Black Bill lined up in my sights.'

'Did you hit any of them?' asked Caleb.

'No, never fired a single shot,' admitted Eli. 'Pity that, I could've claimed the reward an' retired.'

'Maybe you can still retire,' said Caleb. 'Did you see which way they went?'

'South, I reckon,' replied Eli, standing up and showing himself. 'Leastways that's the direction the voice came from.'

'And, as the man said, there's still a long way to go,' said Caleb. 'Can we get down? I don't fancy going through all that undergrowth again.'

'Simple enough,' said Eli. 'It's no more'n fifteen feet.'

'Then let's go,' said Caleb. 'We'd better make sure Miss Greaves is OK.'

'Yeh, I'd almost forgotten about her,' said Eli.

'Let's hope Sioux didn't find her,' said Caleb. 'I'd hate to lose her after all this trouble.'

'So would I,' admitted Eli. 'I allus thought of her as some bitter, interferin' old maid but I gotta admit that she sure has a lot of spunk.'

'Even if she says you smell?'

'Sure, even that,' replied Eli. 'A skunk stinks like hell but I guess he can't smell himself. Same applies to me I guess.'

'Eli,' said Caleb with a knowing laugh, 'if I didn't know better, I'd say you were in love.'

'Don't know about that,' said Eli, 'but she can move into my place any time she has a mind to.'

NINE

They eventually reached the spot where they had left Miss Greaves and, although the horse and mule were still there, Caleb became very worried when there was no sign of her.

'Where is she?' he asked Eli, at the same time drawing his gun. 'Perhaps Sioux found her.'

'Or she's wandered off for some reason,' said Eli. 'It's easy enough to get lost, 'specially somebody what don't know where they are.'

'Miss Greaves!' Caleb called. 'Where are you?'

At first there was no reply and Caleb called again. In the meantime Eli was examining the ground but could not find any signs that anything untoward had occurred. Caleb called again and this time a woman's voice answered.

'No need to shout, Mr Black, I heard you the first time,' she scolded, emerging from behind a large fallen tree and very pleased with herself. 'I've got something to show you.'

Caleb and Eli scrambled over the fallen trunks and stood in amazement at the sight which greeted them.

'Sioux!' exclaimed Caleb.

The half-breed, looking very sullen, was lying on his side with his hands firmly tied behind his back by what appeared to be strands of creepers or vines. Miss Greaves stood on a fallen tree, the pistol in her hand pointing unwaveringly at him.

'He made the mistake of thinking that a frail old woman would be unable to do anything,' she said. 'He's not the first man to make that mistake. I must admit that I was rather fortunate though and that he did have what you call the drop on me. We heard shooting and it put him off guard. He didn't know I had a gun and you should have seen the look on his face when I held it to his head.'

'A very neat job too,' said Eli, examining the strands round Sioux's wrists. 'Where'd you learn that trick?'

'Playing with my brother when we were children,' she said, laughing. 'Well, I think I have done my bit. How did you two fare?'

'Not as well as you,' said Caleb. 'I hit one

of them but they got away. Do you know where his horse is?'

'Don't think he was on a horse,' said Eli. 'I reckon we'll find it down by the basin somewhere.'

'I hope so,' said Caleb. 'We don't want him slowing us down.'

'OK, son,' Eli said to Sioux, 'up you get, looks like you got some more walkin' to do.'

'I'm surprised at you, Eli,' said the half-breed, struggling to his feet. 'Your blood runs through my veins, does that not mean anything to you?'

'You know 'bout that!' grunted Eli. 'I suppose I shouldn't be surprised though. I guess your ma told you.'

'She told me,' snarled Sioux. 'She also told me that you left her when I was only two years old.'

'Sure,' replied Eli, somewhat sadly. 'I just wasn't suited to settlin' down. Anyhow, I figured you'd be better off without me, your ma had family close by.'

'Family!' spat Sioux. 'The fact that I am a half-breed means that I am not welcome by either white man or Indian. It would have been better if you had killed me at birth.'

'I guess it must've been hard for both of you,' said Eli. 'I met your ma once not long after I left but she didn't want anythin' to do with me. Then you moved away further up country. I guessed it was you when you turned up with Black Bill an' it was confirmed by old Sammy Running Deer just before he died.'

'Sammy was the only man who ever accepted me for what I was,' said Sioux. 'Now all my mother's tribe have gone, taken to the reservations by the white man.'

'For their own good,' said Eli.

'For the good of the white man,' snapped Sioux. 'They took land which had belonged to my people for many thousands of years; now they rot, unable to hunt for their food, relying on the white man to feed them. Where is the good in that?'

'That's somethin' I can't do nothin' about,' said Eli. 'Why'd you take up with that no-good Black Bill?'

'Because he and I are the same – despised by the white man.'

'And ended up with a price on your head,' said Caleb. 'Come on, let's get going and hope we find your horse.'

They did find the horse behind some large boulders just off the trail close to the basin. Sioux was placed on it but his hands remained tied. Miss Greaves had made such a good job of tying his wrists that there was no need to change it.

The delay now meant that it would be impossible to reach Beresford that night and Eli told them of an abandoned cabin about two miles south of the woods where they would be safe enough. In the event that Black Bill might attempt to attack them, the cabin was well built and easily defended.

The journey through the woods proved uneventful even if they immediately grabbed at their guns whenever there was a sudden noise. Most of the sounds were made by animals or birds, though there were one or two which defied explanation but which, although obviously uncertain, Eli put down to bears.

'It's either bears or the evil spirits the Indians used to claim haunted these woods,' he said, laughing. 'Since I don't believe in evil spirits I guess it must be the bears.'

'It does not do to mock the spirits,' grumbled Sioux. 'They were here long before the white man.'

Eli proved to be an expert tracker and assured them that the remaining three outlaws were still in front of them. At first he pointed out every little detail but when he realized that his audience was becoming bored with his incessant talking, he gave up. Eventually he pointed along a narrow trail which ran off from the main trail.

'Looks like two of 'em went up there,' he said. 'The other one kept on along this way. Now I wonder why that was? That way leads up to a ridge an' the only way from there is along it. I ain't sure about it after that since I ain't never even been up there myself. Do you know, son?' he asked Sioux.

The half-breed remained silent and sullen and Eli simply shrugged. They continued for about another hour, when they suddenly came to the end of the woods.

Caleb was rather relieved to be out in the open. Quite apart from feeling very uncomfortable in enclosed spaces, he was thankful that the possibility of someone hiding among the trees had disappeared.

'Cabin's down there,' announced Eli half an hour later, pointing at a stone-built cabin about 400 yards away. 'Used to belong to a man from somewhere called Wales who came over to farm sheep. Only trouble was the wolves took more sheep than he could sell to make a livin' so he gave up. He should've asked me, I'd've saved him a whole lot of time an' trouble.'

'Mr Goodman,' said Miss Greaves, shading her eyes and peering at the distant cabin. 'You did say that it was abandoned didn't you?'

'Sure thing ma'am,' said Eli. 'John Evans left more'n five years ago.'

'Well, I could be wrong,' she continued, 'but I do believe there is a horse standing outside.'

'A horse!' exclaimed Eli, also shading his eyes. 'Hell ma'am, you can see a whole lot more'n I can. I can't see nothin'.'

'She's right,' said Caleb. 'There is a horse. Just one, so it can't be Black Bill.'

'Then you both got better eyes than me,' grumbled Eli. 'Maybe I should get some spectacles.'

'You can take our word for it,' said Caleb. 'There is definitely a horse.'

They approached the cabin with extreme caution and when they were about 200 yards away, Caleb suggested that he and Eli should continue on foot.

'Miss Greaves,' he said. 'You and Sioux stay here. You still have the gun, keep him covered and if he makes any attempt to escape, shoot him. Do you think you can do that?'

'Do I shoot to kill?' she asked.

'Only if you have to,' said Caleb. 'If he

does try anything I would suggest that a bullet in his leg would be enough to stop him.'

'It will be a pleasure, Mr Black,' she said.

Caleb and Eli made their way to the cabin on foot, both with guns at the ready and they were both somewhat surprised when their approach remained unchallenged. Eli went round the back and Caleb cautiously went to the front door. Again there was no challenge. Caleb flattened himself against the wall and, after listening for some time, suddenly swung and kicked open the flimsy door.

The expected bullet did not arrive and at first it seemed that the cabin was empty. However, a faint groan from somewhere in the gloom told him that someone was there and that whoever it was was apparently in some pain.

'Don't try anything,' he ordered. 'Stand up and show yourself.'

The response was another groan and by that time Caleb had been joined by Eli. Both men moved slowly towards the sound. They discovered a body lying on what had once been a bed. Eli slowly bent down and examined the body.

'Green!' he announced. 'Saul Green. It

looks like your bullet caused him some damage.'

'He's still alive,' said Caleb. 'He's still breathing.'

'More dead than alive, I'd say,' replied Eli. 'We could do with some light.'

Caleb looked about and found some old paper which he rolled into a torch and lit. Saul Green's shirt was covered in blood and the wound appeared to be in his chest. He pulled Green's shirt apart.

'It looks like he's lost a lot of blood,' said Caleb. 'I knew I'd hit him, in fact I thought I'd killed him. If he's going to stand any chance at all we have to get him to a doctor.'

'Nearest is in Beresford,' said Eli. 'He might not survive the journey.'

'Well we can't leave him here,' said Caleb. 'I'll go and get Miss Greaves, she seems to know a lot of things, perhaps she knows how to stop bleeding. You see if you can get a fire going.'

It appeared that Miss Greaves counted among her other abilities, that of being a nurse. She expertly bandaged the wound using one of her petticoats. In the meantime the half-breed Sioux, was ordered to remain in a corner well away from either the front or back door. Eli succeeded in getting a good fire going and the bed on which Green lay was dragged closer to it.

'There's nothing else I can do for him,' said Miss Greaves. 'My knowledge does not extend to cutting bullets out.'

'At least the bleeding seems to have stopped,' said Caleb. 'All we can do is hope that he survives the night. At least now we know why he split up from the other two.'

'It is strange that you take so much trouble,' said Sioux. 'I would have thought it would not matter to you if he died.'

'It's all a matter of money,' said Caleb with a laugh. 'I'm not sure if the reward holds good if I deliver a dead outlaw.'

'You might make a joke of it,' said Sioux, 'but I suspect it is more than that. Perhaps it is that you feel guilty about shooting him. It is true that you are a minister of the church is it not?'

'I am,' confirmed Caleb, 'but that is not the reason. I have shot and killed quite a few men and have never felt any guilt. Nevertheless, I would never leave a man to die if I could avoid it.'

'And you, Eli, my father, would you leave a man to die?' asked Sioux.

'Nope,' replied Eli. 'But then I ain't never killed a man in my life. In fact I ain't never even shot a man as far as I know.'

'I can believe that,' said Sioux. 'You prefer to abandon women and children.'

Eli grumbled under his breath and went outside. A few minutes later Caleb found him sitting on a stone, his head held in his hands. Eli looked up at Caleb and sighed.

'He's right, damn him,' he said quietly. 'I did abandon him.'

'You did what you thought best at the time,' said Caleb, sitting beside him. 'As to whether or not it was the right decision is purely a matter between you and your conscience.'

'I abandoned both of them,' replied Eli, hoarsely. 'I abandoned him and his ma and now I'm helping to send him to jail. What kind of father does things like that? I just wish to hell that I'd never agreed to help.'

'But you did and you knew about him before you agreed to help,' said Caleb. 'If you felt so strongly, why did you?'

'I guess I thought all that was behind me, it was a long time ago,' said Eli. 'I could've managed if he hadn't known about me I reckon. Or maybe I hoped he would escape. I don't know what I was thinkin'. It didn't seem to matter then.'

'I'm sorry I can't be of more help,' said Caleb.

'Don't suppose you would turn a blind eye if he did...? No, I reckon not, I shouldn't ask,' Eli said, sitting up straighter. 'Anyhow he is a wanted outlaw, ain't no denyin' that fact, so I guess the law has to take its course.'

Caleb returned to the warmth of the cabin but Eli remained outside with his thoughts. Caleb never actually heard him come into the cabin, but he was there when the first rays of light filtered through the rimy window.

The condition of Saul Green appeared to have stabilized during the night. Although still unconscious his breathing seemed easier. Miss Greaves examined the wound and applied clean dressing.

There was no way Green would be able to ride his horse. Even had he been conscious it would have been at least very difficult and probably too dangerous. It was the half-breed, Sioux, who came up with the idea of an Indian-style litter.

This consisted of two long poles fastened at one end to the back of the horse with shorter, more supple branches lashed across lower down. In the absence of string or rope, Miss Greaves's idea of using creepers or vines was adopted. A bed of leaves was laid on the litter and Saul Green placed on it. Miss Greaves elected to ride the horse and pull the litter. Once again, Sioux's wrists were bound, this time using a length of twine which Caleb had in his saddle-bag.

'At least it's open country from here on,' said Eli. 'There's still a few places where Black Bill could ambush us but all we have to do is keep our eyes open.'

'How long will it take?' asked Miss Greaves. 'I am beginning to feel very dirty and very hungry. Yes, I think a good hot bath followed by a decent meal would be most welcome.'

'I ain't so sure about the bath,' said Eli, 'but I'll go along with the meal an' I'll add to that a drink of good whisky. I reckon we should reach Beresford just after noon, barrin' hold-ups that is.'

'Then let's hope that Black Bill has finally given up trying to kill us,' said Caleb. 'He might even have decided that Beresford is not the place to be any longer. That would be a pity though, no Black Bill or Hooper rather diminishes the reward.'

'Perhaps you should give thanks to the Lord that you have survived thus far,' said Miss Greaves. 'I for one am most thankful for your intervention, although I do believe that I would not have been harmed even if there had been no ransom paid.'

'We were goin' to let you go,' said Sioux, with a dry laugh. 'Hoppy wanted to kill you but Black Bill wouldn't hear of it.'

'Then the man does have some spark of decency,' said Caleb. 'Come on, let's get started. I too would appreciate a good bath and a decent meal.'

They had been travelling about two hours when Eli suddenly stopped and listened intently. He silently motioned that they should take cover behind some large boulders a few yards off the trail.

Caleb had to admit that he had not heard a thing but Eli was quite adamant that someone was riding towards them. After about ten minutes Caleb could also hear the unmistakable sound of horses and there seemed to be several of them. Suddenly four riders appeared from round a bend.

'Luke Solomons!' exclaimed Caleb.

'It sure looks like him,' agreed Eli. 'I guess that means we're safe now. Black Bill wouldn't dare take on all of us.'

Eli and Caleb stood up at the same time and waved to the approaching horsemen. Miss Greaves was rather more practical and kept the half-breed covered just in case he should attempt an escape. Sheriff Luke Solomons was plainly surprised to see them and ordered the men with him to watch out for a trap.

'I thought it was about time I came lookin' for you,' he said. 'I've got to admit that I thought you might be dead.'

'As you can see, we're fine,' said Caleb. 'We do have a seriously injured man though, Saul Green.'

'I can see that,' replied the sheriff. 'Good mornin' Miss Greaves,' he continued, touching the brim of his hat. 'Glad to see that you are OK. I see you've got Sioux as well. You have been busy. Where's Black Bill an' Hooper?'

'Couldn't say,' said Eli. 'All we know he was ahead of us.'

'Well we didn't see him,' said the sheriff. 'We were goin' as far as the old cabin. If we hadn't found you by then we were goin' to assume the worst had happened.'

'I see you managed to get some volunteers,' said Caleb.

'I tried to get more,' said Luke, 'but you know how things are.'

The men with the sheriff included Sam Boulton and two whom Caleb did not know. From their actions they were plainly ill at ease, looking about as if expecting to be shot at at any moment.

'OK, Luke,' said one of them, 'so we found 'em. Let's get the hell out of here. This place gives me the jitters.'

'Sure thing,' agreed Luke. 'Are you ready to move?'

'As ready as we'll ever be,' said Caleb. 'I'll tell you what happened as we ride.'

As ever, that strange phenomenon, the bush telegraph, had gone ahead of them and it was obvious the news of their approach to Beresford had reached the town before they arrived, even though they had not seen anyone. The doctor was immediately sent for to examine Saul Green and Sioux was locked in jail. Miss Greaves grandly announced that she was going to have a bath and was not to be disturbed for at least an hour.

As she marched off towards the hotel she was surrounded by inquisitive townsfolk, mainly women, all asking questions at once. Although apparently enjoying her new-found notoriety, she simply held her head high and refused to answer any of their questions.

The doctor announced that he would have to perform an operation to remove the bullet from Green's chest if he was to stand any chance of survival. Even so, he rated the chances of Green even surviving the operation as something well under fifty-fifty. The operation was carried out on a table in the sheriff's office.

Eli Goodman had already taken himself off to the saloon and a bottle of whisky as promised by Caleb. Caleb decided that since there was nothing he could do, he would follow the example of Miss Greaves and have a bath at the barber's shop. As he left, the Reverend Wilberforce met him on the boardwalk.

'Congratulations, Mr Black,' said Wilberforce with more than a hint of derision. 'I must admit that I did not expect to see either you or Miss Greaves again.'

'The Lord was with me,' replied Caleb, quite deliberately adopting a slightly holier-than-thou attitude. 'It was just that He needed some help.'

'I doubt that the Lord needed the assistance of your guns,' replied Wilberforce. 'I suspect that He had the saving of Miss Greaves in hand without your intervention.'

'Possibly, Mr Wilberforce, possibly,' said

Caleb with a broad grin. 'That, however, is something to which we shall never really know the answer. Now, if you will excuse me, I really do need a bath. That is something that even the Lord cannot provide, bountiful though He is.'

'I find your attitude most irreverent, Mr Black,' said Wilberforce. 'In fact I am of the opinion that you are not really an ordained minister. I believe you are using the office as cover for your real business of bounty hunting.'

'Yes, sir,' said Caleb. 'It has proved very useful on more than one occasion, I admit it. Nevertheless, I am what I claim to be and nothing will change that. Good day to you, Reverend. There is a possibility that you will have a funeral at which to officiate quite soon. Saul Green is even now fighting for his life under the knife of the doctor. I suggest that your time would be well spent in praying for him. That is if you consider outlaws worth praying for. Perhaps you place outlaws on a level with negroes, Indians and half-breeds, beyond redemption.'

He did not give the minister time to respond and crossed the street to the barber's shop. He was soon wallowing in a tub of hot water and listening to the almost welcome sound of the constant chatter of the barber.

An hour later he returned to the sheriff's office and discovered that Saul Green had survived the operation but was still in a very serious condition. Miss Greaves too came to see how Green was and was congratulated by the doctor on a job well done. She visibly preened with delight when he assured her that without her intervention Green would have certainly died.

Later, Caleb sought out Eli and discovered him in his cabin, feeling very sorry for himself and plainly the worse for drink. His problem now appeared to be that on seeing his son, Sioux, locked away, he had convinced himself that, as a father, he was a total failure. He also seemed convinced that he had not only failed his son but also himself.

'You made your choice when you walked out on him and his mother,' said Caleb. 'That was many years ago. Nothing can change what happened or the way things have turned out.'

'That's fine for you to say, Reveren',' muttered Eli. 'It ain't your flesh an' blood what you helped send to jail.' He looked up at Caleb, his eyes filled with tears. 'Have you any children?' he asked. Caleb shook his head. 'Then don't preach about somethin' you don't know nothin' about.'

'There's a reward for those men,' said Caleb. 'I'll see that you get your share.'

'Reward!' spat Eli. 'I don't want no damned blood money. You keep it, Reveren', I couldn't touch none of it. There ain't no amount of money can make up for what I did to that boy an' his ma.'

'That's how you feel at this moment, Eli,' said Caleb. 'You'll see things differently when the drink wears off.'

'It won't make no difference though,' said Eli. 'He's still goin' to end up in prison for a good many years, an' I helped put him there.' He glared at Caleb for a few moments. 'Get the hell out of it, leave me to die in my own way.'

Caleb realized that any attempt to reason with Eli at that moment would be a waste of effort and returned to town.

'Well, that's three of 'em,' said Luke when Caleb went to the office. 'I make that six hundred an' fifty dollars. Not what we'd expected but better'n nothin'.'

'I would still like to get my hands on the rest of it,' said Caleb. 'The question now is how? Do you think Black Bill is still around?'

'Not if he has any sense,' said Luke. 'I wouldn't waste my time hangin' about hopin' he'll turn up.'

'No, perhaps I won't,' conceded Caleb.

TEN

Caleb was up a little later than his usual time the following morning, having spent a somewhat restless night. His mind had been on Eli Goodman's reaction to being involved in the jailing of his son. Most unusually, according to Tom Gittins, the owner of the saloon where Caleb was staying, Eli had not been in at all the previous night and, apart from the bottle earlier in the day, had not claimed the bottles of whisky paid for by Caleb.

'I've never known Eli refuse a free drink,' said Gittins. 'He must be ill or somethin'. I know he's an old man an' he has to die sometime, but he's one of those people a man expects to be around for ever.'

'I think I'd better go and check on him,'

said Caleb. 'He certainly wasn't himself yesterday. Give me one of those bottles, it might cheer him up.'

'Sure thing,' said Gittins, fetching a bottle of his best Scotch whisky from behind the bar. 'Is that right that the half-breed, Sioux, is his son?'

'Apparently,' said Caleb. 'At least that's what they both claim.'

'I can't say as I'm too surprised,' said Gittins. 'It was always said that Eli had himself a squaw-woman years ago. That's somethin' quite common with types like Eli. There ain't no white women who go for a man with that kind of life. Still, no matter what Sioux has done, it must be a darned hard thing to do, help send your own flesh and blood to jail.'

'And nobody knows that better than Eli,' said Caleb.

Eli's hovel turned out to be empty. Not only that but the bear he had brought up, Arthur, was also missing. One of the other residents of the tip, a dirty, slovenly woman with an equally dirty child of indeterminate sex clinging to her skirt, called to Caleb as he walked away.

'Eli's gone,' she called. 'He left before dawn, takin' that damned bear with 'im, an' good riddance too, I say. I never felt safe with that thing around. If your name is Caleb Black 'e left a message for you. He says to tell you not to bother lookin' for 'im an' that you'd know what 'e was talkin' about.'

'Thank you,' said Caleb. 'I'm not too surprised.'

'He did that once before, quite a few years ago,' said the sheriff when Caleb told him of Eli's disappearance. 'He was away for about six months then. Most folk thought he'd died or somethin'. Then one day he just turned up again as if it had only been the day before when he left. I expect the same thing will happen this time.'

'He was a lot younger then,' Caleb pointed out. 'Winter will be setting in soon and he might not survive the cold.'

'It's his choice,' said Luke. 'He knows those mountains better'n any man in these parts. There's nothin' either you or I can do about it. It's a free world.'

'No, I suppose not,' agreed Caleb. 'The thing is, he didn't even take any whisky with him. I would have thought in his present state of mind he would have wanted to drown his sorrows.'

'Eli might be a peculiar old man and had a head full of weird ideas sometimes, but he had one rule which he never broke,' said Luke. 'In town he was always drunk, but out there, he never touched a drop. You must've seen that for yourself. Don't you worry about Eli. If he dies out there it will be what he wanted. He always said he'd rather his body feed the buzzards than be buried in the ground.'

Caleb was tempted to go after Eli and attempt to console him, but the more he thought about it the more he could appreciate the old man's point of view. There had been many occasions when he too had felt the need for solitude.

After checking on the condition of Saul Green – which appeared stable for the moment – Caleb met Miss Greaves as she too came to see how Green was. Caleb told her about Eli.

'That's where he belongs,' she said. 'Out there he is master of all he surveys, in town he is nothing. The mountains and the wilderness are his home, towns are a foreign land. He knew that and I believe that is why he took to drink. I wouldn't worry about Mr Goodman. Perhaps he will return one day, perhaps not. Either way it will be what he wants to do.'

'That's what the sheriff says,' said Caleb.

'The thing is, I can't help feeling that I am in some way responsible. It was me who persuaded him to guide me when I went looking for you.'

'If you use that argument,' she said, laughing, 'it is really me who is responsible. After all, was it not me who jabbed that odious man Black Bill with my umbrella? Had I not done so he probably would not have taken me prisoner and you would have had no need to look for me.'

'Point taken, ma'am,' said Caleb. 'I should have known better than try to argue the point with you. I am curious though. Knowing who he was and his reputation, why did you do what you did?'

'At the time I strongly objected to what he was doing,' she said. 'Unfortunately that is the way I am. I do things on impulse. Sometimes it works, sometimes it doesn't. This was one of the occasions it did not.'

'It certainly surprised him though, and the rest of us,' said Caleb.

'Talking of Black Bill,' she said, 'Mrs Casey at the hotel seems to think that he is well away from here by now. Now there's only the two of them Mrs Casey thinks he will just disappear. If he has, it would be a pity because it means somebody else getting

190

the problem. I do hope you had not intended attempting to capture him.'

'It had crossed my mind,' admitted Caleb. 'The sheriff seems to think that he's probably gone as well. If that is the case, I suppose I might as well move on. There's nothing to keep me in Beresford any longer. I know the Reverend Wilberforce will be only too glad to see the back of me. I get the distinct impression that he does not like me.'

'Another odious man,' said Miss Greaves. 'A minister he may be, but there is something about that man which I do not trust. He says one thing one day and another thing the next. I know he also has a low opinion of me, but that is because I rarely attend any of his services. Frankly, his sermons are just about the most boring I have ever heard.'

'You haven't heard mine,' said Caleb, with a broad grin.

'I think you could be very interesting, Mr Black,' she said. 'I did hear a black preacher once, a long time ago, and he was surprisingly uplifting. Mr Wilberforce's sermons can send anyone to sleep.'

'I have yet to find anyone who actually likes the man,' said Caleb. 'I suppose his wife must.'

'I wouldn't be too certain of that,' she said. 'She's as bad as him. To her, appearance is more important than anything and I think she would rather appear as the minister's wife in some larger town or city than Beresford. Somewhere where she can play the lady bountiful and rub shoulders with the rich and powerful. Perhaps you should set up here in Beresford, I'm quite certain that you would acquire quite a following.'

'Including yourself?' asked Caleb.

'Yes, *Reverend,*' she said. 'Even me.'

'It's a tempting thought,' admitted Caleb. 'I have been giving more and more thought to retiring from bounty hunting of late. I'm getting no younger and one of these days somebody is going to prove to be that little bit faster on the draw than I am. But no, and coming from you I find the suggestion most flattering, I do not believe that this is the right town nor the right time.'

'A pity,' she said. 'By the way, I never did thank you for rescuing me. Thank you.' She stood on tiptoes and kissed his cheek. 'There, I've done something I thought would be impossible, I've kissed a negro.'

'My pleasure, ma'am,' said Caleb with a broad grin. 'My pleasure, although I did have my doubts at times.'

Quite suddenly, a youth rode into town, calling for the sheriff. The youth reined his horse to a stop outside the office and almost fell off it. He dashed into the office and a few seconds later Luke was running out.

'Ted,' he called to his deputy who was walking across the street. 'Get Sam Boulton, Greg Harrison, Chad Brookes and anyone else you can find. There's a fire out at the Musgrove farm.'

'Can I help?' asked Caleb.

'No need for you to bother, Reverend,' panted Luke. 'This don't need a gun. My guess it's old Granny Musgrove what's set the fire goin'. She's done it a couple of times before. Anyhow, Ted's takin' you to the bank when it opens to collect your money an' James Sylvester don't like bein' kept waitin' especially when he's openin' just so's he can pay you out.'

'Opening just for me?' queried Caleb as the sheriff ran to get his horse.

'It would appear so, Mr Black,' said Miss Greaves. 'It is Saturday and the bank does not normally open on a Saturday except when the cattle drives are on.'

'At least I'm as important as a cow,' said Caleb.

The call to attend the fire at the Musgrove

farm drew more volunteers than the call to form a posse had done. In fact Caleb counted at least twelve men riding out. Miss Greaves noted the fact as well.

'I see the good citizens of Beresford are rallying to the help of a neighbour,' she said with a knowing smile. 'That is how it should be I suppose. I might be getting cynical in my old age, but I can't help but wonder if the fact that Granny Musgrove just happens to brew the finest cider in the West has anything to do with it. There will be a few thick heads tonight.'

'Cynical, ma'am, you?' said Caleb with a broad grin. 'Perish the thought.'

With the sheriff and a large number of the men gone, the town became strangely quiet, almost too quiet for Caleb's liking. He could not put a finger on it, but he felt a strange sense of foreboding. Everything appeared normal and the few people he met seemed happy enough. The subject of Eli Goodman cropped up a few times but everyone seemed convinced that he had simply taken himself off on one of his trips into the wilderness and that there was no need to be concerned.

It was about an hour after the sheriff and the volunteers had left for the Musgrove farm that Caleb's sense of foreboding became even greater. He tried to convince himself that it was all in his imagination but the feeling persisted. Suddenly, his feelings were proved correct.

A lone horseman galloped into town and dashed into the sheriff's office. Caleb, who was close by, followed the man inside.

'Black Bill!' said the man. 'He's headed this way. Black Bill and Hooper.'

'How far?' asked the deputy.

'Maybe a mile,' panted the man. 'Where's the sheriff?'

'Out at the Musgrove farm,' said Ted. 'Seems Granny Musgrove has set fire to the place again.'

'All very convenient,' said Caleb. 'How far is this Musgrove farm?'

'About twenty minutes' hard ride,' said the deputy.

'Too convenient,' said Caleb. 'I suspect that Granny Musgrove is not the one responsible for the fire on this occasion. I think that Black Bill set fire to the place just to get Luke out of the way. I believe that his target is me.'

'Except that he wasn't to know that you wouldn't go with them,' said Ted.

'That was a chance he had to take,' said Caleb.

'Sam,' the deputy said to the man, 'get yourself out to the Musgrove place as fast as you can. Tell the sheriff that he has to get back here in double quick time.'

'Sure thing,' gasped Sam. 'I don't want to be around when Black Bill gets here.'

'You're probably right about him wanting you,' said Ted as Sam rode out. 'What you goin' to do about it?'

'Be here when he turns up,' said Caleb. 'I'd hate to disappoint him. This is between him and me, there's no need for you to become involved.'

'I'll be standin' by just in case,' said Ted. 'I ain't no gunman an' I know I wouldn't stand a chance but I can't just stand by an' watch.'

'Thanks,' said Caleb, 'but don't put yourself in any danger.'

Caleb took up position outside the sheriff's office and it seemed that word had already spread throughout the town since almost everyone had suddenly disappeared. Caleb did not have too long to wait.

Two horsemen slowly approached the town and Caleb allowed them to advance to within about fifty yards of the office before standing up and walking into the middle of the street. He flipped the right side of his coat to one side to reveal one of his guns, the other side he kept covered.

This was a tactic that had often worked for him in the past. Most people assumed that he only had the one gun. He did not know if Black Bill or Hooper knew any different and he had to assume that they did not.

For some time the three men looked at each other in silence, as if each were waiting for another to react first. Eventually Black Bill nudged his horse forward a few yards.

'We meet again,' said Black Bill, slouching in his saddle and staring at Caleb. 'I ain't never killed a black brother before, but I guess there's always a first time for everythin'.'

'Black I might be,' said Caleb. 'Brother I am not. Do you think you can take me? I don't have the same problem as you, Mr Williams, I have killed black men before. It's no different to killing a white man, they both bleed red blood.'

'I can believe that,' said Black Bill. 'You is what I call a white black man, scum of the earth, a traitor to your own kind.'

'And you should recognize scum,' goaded Caleb. 'You've lived with it for so long it's part of you. I suppose that reasoning makes your friend a traitor to his own kind as well.'

Black Bill laughed and dismounted. Hoppy Hooper remained in his saddle and did not seem quite as confident as his companion.

'Go ahead, Mr Preacher,' said Black Bill. 'Call me all the names you can think of, it's the last chance you is goin' to get. I hear that you think you're pretty fast with that gun. Only thing is, I'm faster.'

'We shall see,' said Caleb. 'It seems to me that I have heard those very same words before. The thing is I am still here, those who claimed to be faster are not. As you say though, there is a first time for everything.'

'A first an' last time as far as you're concerned,' sneered Black Bill.

'I think I am right in assuming that the fire out at the farm was started by you,' said Caleb.

'Somethin' like that,' admitted Black Bill. 'Now, Mr Preacher, I say again, I hear tell that you fancy yourself as somethin' of a gunman, an' I repeat, I got news for you, you just met somebody who is a whole lot faster.'

'I'm surprised at you facing a man direct,' said Caleb. 'I would have thought a bullet in the back was more your style.'

'Sometimes it is, sometimes it ain't,' said

Black Bill. 'This is one of them times it ain't. I want to see the fear in your eyes.'

Black Bill slowly moved away from his horse and stood, legs slightly apart, facing Caleb. Hoppy Hooper slowly drew his gun and waited.

'I see, if you don't get me, he will,' said Caleb. 'The thing is you might never live to see if he does or not.'

'I think they call it insurance,' said Black Bill.

'And this is what I call insurance!'

Black Bill and Hooper looked to their right to see Miss Greaves standing on the boardwalk with a rifle at her shoulder. She slowly moved out, keeping the rifle trained on Hoppy Hooper. She was about thirty yards away from the two men, far enough away for their pistols to be very inaccurate against her but they were well within range of the rifle.

'Bitch!' snarled Black Bill. 'I should have killed you while I had the chance. That's what Hoppy wanted to do.'

'We all make mistakes, Mr Williams,' she said. 'Now, Mr Hooper, put that gun back and don't interfere. I can assure you that I am a very good shot.' Hooper grunted something which was very uncomplimentary to Miss Greaves and certainly questioned the legitimacy of her birth, but obeyed the instruction. 'Now, Mr Williams, I think the next move is up to you.'

Black Bill laughed and slowly edged back towards his horse. On reaching it he was out of sight of Miss Greaves and her rifle. It seemed that he was about to mount the horse but, as he turned towards it, he suddenly swung round.

It was questionable whether it was Black Bill or Caleb who fired first. Whichever of them it was, it was certainly Black Bill who tumbled to the ground. Caleb remained upright. Hoppy Hooper had snatched at his gun and fired at Miss Greaves but, as expected, the bullet went wide. Miss Greaves might have been a little slow in reacting but when she did her shot was accurate and Hooper fell from his horse. The animals shied away, leaving both men exposed.

Black Bill rose slightly and aimed at Caleb but Caleb's second shot was extremely accurate in that it smashed into Black Bill's hand, sending his gun spinning across the dusty street. Hoppy Hooper remained where he was, apparently lifeless.

'Nice work, Miss Greaves,' said Caleb. 'I

thank you.'

'I'm simply repaying a debt, Mr Black,' she said as she stepped off the boardwalk. She was still taking no chances and held the rifle at the ready, covering both men on the ground. 'You saved my life, I've saved yours.'

Caleb too went to the two outlaws. Black Bill was certainly still alive and had apparently taken the first bullet in his upper chest. His hand was shattered, exposing a few broken bones. He bent down to examine Hoppy Hooper and discovered that he too was still alive.

'I think you'd better call a doctor,' said Caleb.

'I suggest that we get them in jail first,' said Miss Greaves.

'Not for them, for me,' grimaced Caleb. 'Black Bill was right, he was a good shot.' He tried to raise his arm and grunted in pain. 'It looks and feels like my shoulder is broken or even worse.'

By that time Deputy Sheriff Ted and two other men were rushing across the street. Ted managed to catch Caleb as he suddenly collapsed.

'Your shoulder bone is damaged, but it's

nothing more than a chip,' announced the doctor. 'I've taken the bullet out, you should be fine in a couple of weeks.'

'Thanks Doc,' said Caleb. 'I thought I was a goner when I collapsed. That's the closest to death I've ever come.'

'There was no chance of you dying, so don't try to make more of it than it was,' assured the doc. 'It was just the shock which made you collapse. It's quite common. I'm just surprised that you were able to stand upright at all.'

'I never felt a thing,' said Caleb. 'The first I knew about it was when I saw the blood. Then it started to hurt, really hurt. What about the other two?'

'First things first,' said the doc. 'Looking after you was far more important than either of them. Now you're dealt with I can take a look at them. I don't think either of them are that bad though, but it will be a long time before Black Bill uses his right hand again, if at all.'

Caleb looked about, realized that he was on the table in the sheriff's office and saw Luke Solomons and Miss Greaves.

'Tell the bank president I'm sorry I couldn't keep the appointment,' he said. 'Unfortunately I was unavoidably delayed.'

202

'He said to tell you that there's no hurry,' said Luke.

'Well there's nothing else I can do for him,' said the doc. 'The best place for him is in bed for a few days.' He looked sternly at Caleb. 'And don't get any ideas about thinking you know better. I'll call in to see you tonight. Now, it would appear that I have other patients waiting and I think I am going to need this table again.' Caleb made a move to get off the table but was held down by the doc. 'You might be a big man, Reverend, but I can't allow you to walk. Luke, get some men to carry him. Another thing, Reverend, no alcohol, at least not for twenty-four hours. In my experience wounds such as you have and alcohol do not mix.'

Caleb sank back and grinned. 'That's a pity,' he said. 'I really fancied a good whisky.'

It was three days before the doctor would allow Caleb out of bed and he was almost sorry. He was just beginning to acquire a taste for being waited on. Nevertheless, once he was up and about, he was anxious to be on his way.

Black Bill and Hoppy Hooper had survived their operations and arrangements had been made for their transport to the state penitentiary. Two days after being allowed out of bed, Caleb picked up the $1,600 reward. As promised, he offered Sheriff Luke Solomons half.

'No, Reverend,' said the sheriff. 'You made that offer on the basis that I was goin' to help you catch them. I didn't do a damned thing. If anyone should share in it, it must be Eli Goodman an' Miss Greaves. Hell, I sure would like that kinda money, but since I didn't earn it, I wouldn't feel comfortable taking it.'

'I did offer Eli a share,' said Caleb, 'but he refused and now he's disappeared. Perhaps you are right about Miss Greaves though. If it hadn't been for her I might well be dead now.'

'She's a very surprisin' woman,' said Luke. 'While you've been in bed she's had at least four offers of marriage that I know of.'

'Has she accepted any of them?'

'Better ask her,' said Luke. 'She's comin' across the street now.'

'Mr Black,' said Miss Greaves when asked about the proposals of marriage. 'I have been a spinster all my life and I do not intend taking on a man at my age. Apart from one unfortunate experience, I have always managed to keep men at arm's length and see little point in allowing any man into my bed at my time of life. Besides, the one idea all the men who have proposed seem to have is someone to keep house, cook and clean for them. Since it has been many years since I performed such functions even for myself, I have no intention of starting again now for a man.'

'Very wise,' said Caleb. 'I have thought about taking a wife a few times, but to me one of the purposes of getting married is to have children. I think I am a bit too old for that now. Now, Miss Greaves,' he continued, 'had it not been for you, I could well be occupying a plot in the Reverend Wilberforce's cemetery now. I have just been paid quite a lot of money for those outlaws and I feel that I ought to share it with you.'

'Most kind of you, Reverend,' she replied. 'However, as you have no doubt heard, I am quite a wealthy woman. Most certainly I have far more money than I shall ever need or spend so I do not need any more. Besides, I have just had a most exciting experience. In fact it was the most exhilarating I have had since being involved with some Texas Rangers and a shipment of gold at the end of the war.'

'You certainly seem to have led an interesting, active life,' said Caleb.

'I certainly have, Mr Black, and I have very few regrets. There is little I would change. I dare say both you and I have quite a few tales to tell.'

'Perhaps we can get together one day and exchange a few,' said Caleb.

'I think not, Reverend,' she said. 'This is the parting of the ways as far as we are concerned.'

Caleb rode out of Beresford shortly before dawn the following morning. There was nobody to witness his departure and that, like Eli Goodman, was the way he liked it; no fuss, no farewells.